I0716385

This edition first published in 2023
by New West/ Wild Fire Publishing
103-955 Humboldt St. Victoria B.C. V8V 2Z9

ISBN 978-1-7389680-3-9

"The Heavy Metal Sound of Steel", was originally published in Fleas on the Dog, Issue 4, October 2019. "The Book of John, pt. 1 'The Curse of John'" was originally published in Crack the Spine, issue 221, August 2017.

First Things Last

First Things Last

Stories

Daniel J. Thompson

New West/
Wild Fire
Publishing

Table of Contents

When Tragedy Strikes

O ut of all the stories that get picked, the most interesting are the ones with the possibility of danger. He didn't know what kind of character he was until tragedy struck.

Animist Girlfriend

There's her and then there's the rest of the world. At any given moment, she is the only thing that is real. Asserting the independence of her will through sudden movements, the way one would come up with a joke, or a point of contention, "I'm doing things with my arms, *they're mine*" waving them in front of herself, marking the boundary between her world and everyone else's. A threshold that although it can be crossed, cannot be conquered, taken or destroyed.

No one will know what it is like to be her, just as she will never know what it is like to be anyone else. But the instrument is only as good as the observer, the subject of its own observation, because there can be no measurement without observation and no observation without measurement.

'A door through which the whole world passes...' is how she often refers to herself, sensitive to a fault, especially when interpreting danger. Detecting sounds and smells that might not even be there.

Other times she doesn't seem to notice the world at all. So much a part of it that the passing of time and space never occurs to her. Seconds blend into hours into days, as if there were no point of demarcation.

"Behind you," to a bee on the sidewalk. Thanking the elevator as she gets out on the third floor, "force of habit." The way one does while deplaning, or getting off a bus as if to show one's gratitude for reaching their destination alive, but when it's over and their safety is assured, goes back to taking it, and everything else, for granted. She, however, never takes her safety for granted and is the safest person I know.

Arrivederci, do svidaniya, auf wiedersehen, vaya con dios, hasta la vista, sayonara and let's not forget *Adios.* Every goodbye is a hello to something else; hello closet, hello car, hello home. Turning her back on what's behind in order to face what she's heading towards, while the world itself never responds aside from its disappearance from our immediate attention, because for it there is only one response: *I am. I am when you're opening the door, I am when you're walking down the street, I am in the trees, I am in the sky. I am on the day you were born and I am on the day you will die.*

"Thanks for the ride," she says.

"What do you mean?" I say, "we're both going to the same place."

"Not you... Cammy."

Cammy, the Camaro.

I suggest that she thank the street while she's at it, but she says her feet already do that. The one affirming the other.

"What about toilets?"

"Institutional toilets don't count," she says.

"I think if a thing does a job, it deserves a thank you. You can't just thank one thing and not another if they're doing the same job."

She sits there with a distant look on her face. Eyes focused on a spot just in front of her as if it were a circus of atoms in spin.

"What? What did I say?"

"I know they're just things, you don't have to remind me of that. It's the thing in itself."

"The thing in itself?"

"What makes it one thing and not another; *a basis in that which does not change*", she says as if quoting a famous person. "Only once something has a name does it become real for us... and they *know it* because the *idea* is *their* group identity. They may not be alive, but the idea *is*."

"Who said that?"

"I did."

She says that although she is an animist, she doesn't believe that all things are alive, but are simply extensions of the absolute.

"In the beginning there was One thing. Then somehow, the One thing separated and then there were three; Time, Space and Eternity; The Father, the Son and the Holy Ghost. Space being the shared surface that unites them and pulls them apart."

In a way we're all like my girlfriend, the girlfriend of the moment, or 'the One', definitive version to which all others must compare.

Although she does not say as much, I think I'm starting to see things the way she does, uncontaminated by the rest of the world.

Her body composed of the same parts as mine, plus a few others, which seem to matter so much more, that is, if you think of her as an object... Her world of ideas conceivable to the rest of us only as products, patents, shares, taking up space in warehouses and the cluttered shelves of homes.

They can't speak, but does that mean they don't have anything to say? They know things we'll never know. Of their relationships to each other... of what they are in themselves.

Each thing being equally important, whether alive or dead, past or present, animate or inanimate.

"We made objects, but what made us? Objects have a purpose, therefore we must as well."

Now that we have objects, we can't go back to not having them. We make them because we must. It's what we do.

Thank you for getting us this far... now it's time for us to help you.

But it could also go the other way. That we have more than we know what to do with. That they are taking over our lives. Because after a certain point, we don't own them anymore, they own us.

At the building, we have to go through the outer door in order to get to the inner door of our apartment. She gets there first and waits outside.

"Don't you have your keys, or do you expect the door to open by itself?"

"Not always. You have to wait your turn."

I unlock the door.

"Hello, house," she announces.

Everything is the way we left it.

"Do you think all this stuff exists even when we're not looking at it?"

"There is always something looking at it."

"Who? God?"

"Everything is looking at everything else and together they make up the One."

"Is the One, a thing?"

"It is an experience that is having us as much as we are having it."

I can't deny what she says, not only because I can barely wrap my head around it, but because it seems to have wrapped itself around me.

She's always finding things and giving them away; furniture, clothes, paintings. A minimalist collector of junk and debris, caught in a double bind of preventing waste, but also of conserving what's already made.

Redeeming the cast-off detritus of the world through an appreciation of what went into making them.

Books she says are different, their lives are transitory, existing somewhere between idea and thing, content and form. When they say, 'this book' they don't *just* mean this book, the glue and paper, but the ideas, the 'glue' that sticks them together, along with the letters and *numbers*, which are an emanation of something realer still. Elevated above the things to what is behind them, just as a group of nine things does not exhaust the idea of nine. The number nine is always there, regardless of what it is counting or how many times it is used.

It is only in isolation that the number of objects matter, while in the world outside, we never seem to notice numbers. Each thing blending into the other as if thrown upon one great compost heap. The final form contained in its essence, the metals; gold, copper, iron, lead. The elements; earth, air, fire and water.

There is a reliability of objects that does not extend outside the home, where things are constantly shuffled off, moved around, used up, lost or turned into something else. Moving amoung them as they move amoung us. What we go into and come out of. Waves crashing against the shore, this moment, this day into the next.

Forgetting, as we watch it going on around us, who we are or where we've been, until we're there again, in a certain place, at a certain time.

Relieved when we find that it's the same as we remember it, and in a way, as it remembers us.

Animist Girlfriend

She embraces it all in one gesture, in one word,
thanks.

Revenant Girlfriend (Waterslides in Auxiliary Dormitory Washroom pt. 1)

We're on our fourth or fifth date (the fifth if you consider the first one a date), arriving at her place around 9:00. It's a girl's dorm up on university heights. Almost a half-hour bus ride from downtown.

After a bit of kissing and vigorous rubbing she says she has to go to bed.

Bed as in her bed, alone. She isn't allowed to have guests past 11:00, especially male guests.

"I didn't know anyone did that anymore," I say.

"Well, it's the rule. And until I can afford a place of my own, it's what I have to do."

"Why don't you come back to my place?"

"I have to study, and besides, rules are rules."

"I'll go then. I just need to use the washroom."

"I don't have one in here," gesturing to the four walls and not much else.

"That's too bad."

"At least I don't have a roommate."

"There's that," I say, lingering a little.

"You can use the washroom down the hall, but you have to hurry, you only have *ten minutes*."

"I'll be quick."

She purses her lips, "give me a kiss."

I lean in, one hand in the dip of her back, the other on the side of her face.

"But just a small one, *remember* you only have *ten minutes*."

I give her a peck, no saliva, "can I call you tomorrow?"

"You may text me before three and call any time after five and before eleven."

"So, six?"

"Six o'clock is fine."

She says the washroom is five doors down on the right, almost to the end of the hall.

"How many washrooms are on this floor?" I say.

"Two… but they're communal."

"If they're communal how can I use them?"

"There's a gender-neutral washroom, for guests, but it's only open until 11:00."

"Those are some pretty strict rules."

"Those are the rules. Now go, *hurry*."

It's large for a guest washroom, with one fogged up window, a small toilet stall and three large tubes where urinals should be, wide enough to crawl through, to sit upright, to kneel, like the ones that vent air in hospitals, rise out of the roof and bend at right angles in the open air.

A toilet flushes in another part of the building. The sound draws nearer, impossibly close, trickling down the inside of my skull. I put my ear to the wall. Water falls along the long axis of my body and passes through the floor, dragging my bladder, seized in an uncontrollable urge to urinate. I step toward one of the tubes, tugging at my waistband in preparation of a flood.

The janitor rushes in and tries to stop me. He wants me to pay a toll.

I give him the slip, slide through one of the tubes.

The streets are quiet, asphalt glistening beneath a light pattering of rain. I look down to see that I'm carrying a red jerry can, the liquid sloshing around inside as if it is trying to get out. A purpose, whatever it is, more immediate than mine.

I open the door to my apartment, sensing something different. As if someone is already here and *I* am coming into *its* space; an atmosphere of sitting, relaxing in cranial depressurization for the remainder of time that seems to stand still.

I pick up the phone, but instead of a dial tone there's a loud hiss, like the receiver is filling with water, spraying out the speaker and mic holes.

Movement catches in the corner of my eye; a shape darker than the rest of the room. Jittering in the raster scatter of the television and chattering of voices in feigned, forced calm, reaffirming an absolute state of ordinary, holding back the darkness for another night.

The shadow turns toward me, dispelling every consoling thought of self, memory, home, until I become a part of it. That in some way, I know what it knows. A recognition like being in the same room as myself, or the antithesis of myself. A part that wants to wipe the other part out. Erase its existence so it can take over.

With what awareness I still have, I imagine a light, flowing up and out, like a waterfall. Foam sparks and mist filling the space as the shadow grows darker. Taking human form because it knows what scares me the most.

"You mustn't be afraid. I'm here to protect you from the other ones. I was told they were bothering you."

"*Who* told you?"

"I believe it was you, or it could've been someone else?"

"What do you want?"

"Give me a drink."

I give him the gas can. Two holes appear in its body; one on top of the other, becoming perfectly round as they turn to look straight at me or through me. It's eyes becoming my eyes, interpreting what I otherwise could not, in the same way that it could crush me if it wanted to; a fearsome and powerful entity, but its power is also my power. Feeling it already, as I wrestle it to the floor. The strength draining out of it with every push and pull until it is as light as an umbrella, folding it up and slipping it into its vinyl sleeve.

Once it is contained, I let it back out and flick on the light, losing track of it amoungst the traceries, vibrating nearly as fast as the light and therefore, indistinguishable from it.

I grab the gas can, still quite full and head out into the hall. I hear the neighbors shuffling around behind their doors, sliding chains into housings and deadbolts, wondering what I'm doing out here, if I'm the monster that they fear.

The building becomes transparent to thought; some kind of hyper-dimensional construct experiencing a break down or contradiction, as in the same matter occupying the same space. The skin of reality come peeling off to reveal the operations behind smooth exterior walls made more permeable to waves, light. The whole building visible from any point inside or out, openwork steel girders bowed like the struts of a barrel or cask.

The elevator is just an empty shaft partitioned off by glass. The door slides open with the hiss of air escaping a vacuum. There are several other people already 'on board'. Each looking like they got on in a different place, if not a different world.

Something releases as the platform begins to rise. Horizontal bands of colour blur past in streaks of green, gray, blue and brown; lights on a busy street, enchanted islands offshore at dawn, snow on giant cedars.

An old man emphatically gestures, "Don't try to stand, just sit down."

My lungs empty out from vertigo and a lack of oxygen as we continue our ascent. Refocusing my eyes on the people around me. I had forgotten about them. Like we were all looking through the same set of optics.

The elevator stops at the top of a cliff overlooking the ocean; broad, flat and blue. A whale has washed up on shore, I can hear it singing, a language deeper than mind, deeper than soul.

I climb down, feet sinking into sand as I stand before its gaped mouth.

Baleen screen door admits insects.

O! Beached whale, how beautiful you sing... The last of its knowledge seeping out in a hiss, catches my ears and I see... The water it was born in, the family that it knew. Its home in the narrow channels and caves. Lights where there should be no light. Air where there should be no air. Continents like islands. Centuries in the blink of an eye. High tide washing it out to sea cemetery.

When I get back to the top, I join, or am joined by, 'the teacher'. Manipulating the environment through metaphors. Parallax prospectus of mental pictures *pro specere* the future. Flipping through photographs held up to the sky, taken from different angles, heights, POV of a bird in flight.

"Did you bring what I asked for?"

"Yes," handing him the gasoline.

He takes a drink and hands it back with a gesture that says, now ask me what you've wanted to know.

"How do I get her back?" I say.

He purses his lips, breath smelling of petrol.

I move in close, imagining her as our lips touch and suddenly I'm falling back through layers of cycles of earth, air, water, fire... until I reach my destination.

She answers on the third knock, "didn't you find it? It's the last door on the..." cutting her off with a kiss, "...right, you better hurry or he'll find you."

"He already did."

She loses the concerned look, "you found him, and now you've come for me."

After the other two, I wonder if she'll be harder.

"We are the ones we've been waiting for," a password of some kind, opening the gates, slipping through portal after portal. Knowing things that I couldn't have known, seeing things I couldn't have seen. Three becoming one until I don't know who or where I am, drifting into sleep or another life.

When I wake up, I'm in my own bed. I call her just to see if she's real, then I remember, not before 6:00, "oh shit," I say and quickly hang up.

Texting, *sorry, I forgot, I just wanted to say hi.*

She responds, *In class. Call later.*

I check the apartment for any signs of last night and get ready for work. It's an office job, cubicles spread out in an otherwise empty floor. I say hi to Max and Darcy as I head to my little corner of productivity. Checking emails and starting in on the days to-do list, a lot like yesterday's, remembering in pieces the night before. Not quite a dream, but not quite real. I wonder if I'll ever see her again. Or was she there just to teach me a lesson, maybe one day I'll get it right I tell myself. *We are the ones we've been waiting for...*

*How Yankee Doodle Got a Feather in His Hat
(or, The Origin of 'the Dude')*

It's a familiar story, Yankee Doodle, one of those early pioneers of the North American continent, who dared to create something that had never before existed in a world where there was nothing new under the sun, but in America; the land of the setting sun, there was always the chance that the sun would rise again, anew.

Born Walter Shakermaker, the character known as Yankee Doodle was a British nobleman, although he believed his real parentage to be of Italian nobility and frequently wrote letters to the Vatican and the Baron of Italy using his mother's maiden name Ricci, inquiring into his genealogical records. The closest he came was a family in Naples who shared a second cousin, but the cousin was British.

As it turns out though, being of noble birth did not necessarily predispose one to being either stylish, or clean. Stories of Louis the XIV's offensive body odour are notorious. His majesty had only taken a total of *two* baths from birth 'til the time of his death from dysentery.

Shakermaker, however, was a 'neat' person, having traveled extensively in Europe and the near East, where he became fluent in the latest styles, but his ignorance of the culture, namely the Italian, was obvious to everyone on the continent, as if breeding and refinement could be achieved as easily as sticking a feather in one's cap, thereby raising oneself to a higher status; a higher elevation of coiffure. What was generally referred to as a Macaroni, a doodle or more commonly, a dandy.

Of course, no one in America knew the difference between a doodle and a dandy, so the name stuck, as there weren't that many dandies in America at the time. The more common name for such a person was 'egghead', 'pouf' or 'fop', which is of course, what the Americans took him for, rather than a man of good breeding and taste.

Though misunderstood, he was widely respected and soon adulated by his many fans and imitators. Transforming their rugged appearance with a little plumage, collar and cologne.

Like Orpheus, Don Quixote or Johnny Appleseed before him, he fertilized the ground he walked on, bringing a mixture of culture and tradition to the

New World through inspired dishes using whatever ingredients he could find and importing from Europe what he couldn't. Including the renowned 'King of Cheese' *Parmigiano-Reggiano*, various nuts, seeds, dried fruits, olive oil, pasta and even live snails and herbs like basil, to be cultivated in summer gardens by specially trained gardeners until enough of the spice could be produced to go around. Mixing the native garlic, parsley and thyme he first made a sauce, then, using the cheeses of the domesticated bison, threw together such a dish as was never heard of or tasted again.

The Americans, unable to distinguish between the various shapes and sizes of noodles and pairings of sauces, simply referred to them as macaroni, though properly speaking they weren't.

A simple substitution or change in cut and size of noodle could throw off a whole recipe and thus spawn a totally unique dish or style of cuisine. Proper macaroni consisting of a tubular noodle cut to the size of a die or phalanges (bone of the hand) baked with one of three types of cheese and fresh milk is the traditional macaroni dish.

Shakermaker served provisionally in the war of 1776 as mess cook and personal chef to General Tomkins and Watt. Tomkins, being especially impressed with the quality of food he was able to produce from just a few herbs and otherwise bland pastry of egg yolks and flour, procured him as his personal chef.

He never saw battle, but always carried his matched pair of muskets, so that in addition to being a soldier, he was a gentleman and a scholar. Assumed to be just as inept at marksmanship as he was at any other sort of *manship*, his opponents would indulge him in his folly, but Yankee Doodle was a crack shot and his detractors soon became few and far between. So much so, that soldiers removed in time and space, honoured the man with a song recited to the tune of a jaunty march, usually featuring the flute and snare drum, though fiddles and horns were sometimes were used.

While the man Shakermaker was just another soldier, the legend of Yankee Doodle continues to this day, depicting the valorous actions of this once great man as bumptious yokel, haphazardly putting a feather in his hat and so falsely dubbing it Macaroni. However, it was not Shakermaker who was the bumptious yokel, but the Americans that Shakermaker tried to ennoble through the lively stories and cuisine of the Mediterranean and beyond.

Though no longer referred to as doodles or dandies, the term dude was and is still used in the same way, popularized by the youth culture of the late 1800's to describe pretty much anyone under the age of forty who didn't know or couldn't find their ass with both hands. *Dude where're my undergarments, Dude who ate the last piece of lasagna, Dude what ever happened to asking before you borrow my wig.* I doubt whether any of these young people can tell you the true history of the OD 'Original Dude', their namesake and patron saint. Nothing remaining of this esteemed personage but micro-waved noodles and the apocryphal feather in the hat, as these and more timeless traditions are lost at an alarming rate, while so-called hipsters and urban cowboys profess rugged manliness simply by growing a beard and wearing a shirt of plaid or tweed, not so. Ample research is required before blindly appropriating the hard-won traditions of our predecessors. It is both ignorant and rude, and an affront to the values and sacrifices that made and continue to make this country great.

The Meaning of Orange

A buzzer rings somewhere outside. Proximate noon tips over the eaves, putting the room in the path of the sun for the rest of the day. Curt often dreams of building a wall, some kind of fortification or deterrent that would seal him off from the outside, but all that would do is keep him in, which is exactly what he wants.

Trees posture defiantly, higher than any wall or authority to cut them down.

He sits in the same position for most of the day, every day. Time measured by the angle of light, the way his ancestors did for millennia; the oblique angles of winter, the acute angles of summer.

A slant of light falls across his face. He doesn't draw the blinds because that would admit defeat. Enduring the rays of ultraviolet crossing incomprehensible distances of space with the capability to burn, singe and sear flesh. The fact that he can't look at it reminds him of God; a being so powerful that if we were to look at it, he would go blind.

He reaches out, smearing grease from his cheek into his eye with the swipe of a careless hand. Three nights a week he passes out in the purple armchair by the window. The rest of the time he wakes up in his room on the second floor, laid out on top of the bed as if all he was was his clothes.

Shutting his eyes against the pain, he brings his hands back down to his lap, flexing them in and out of fists. The first in a series of rituals to be performed in a certain order: combing and then gelling his hair while it is still wet. Smooth in the back, high in the front. Waiting for it to dry and then going over it again with the spray. Noting the time on the clock with an erasable pen and then flipping the cushion on his chair to the previous day's side before leaving the house. Locking the door behind him, then checking to see if it's locked, but going back anyway to make sure the oven is off. Forbidding himself from checking again, as he navigates the maze of topiaries crowding the garden path to where it comes out at the gate, pausing to make sure the way is clear before proceeding.

Shoes scuffing crab-wise, sidestepping cracks, bubblegum, dog doodie before falling into his stride. Indecisively taking one step back for every two steps forward so it appears as if he is walking in the direction he just came as much as the way he is going. The tuft of bangs spiked up in the front, bounces in rhythm to his steps, giving the impression that he is not only moving both forward and back but also sideways… to the end of the block where the crossing guard is holding her big red lollipop sign. Though her job is to be impartial, she has been known to favor even a single pedestrian over a queue of idling cars. Smiling to everyone indiscriminately, Curt included, who returns her smile like a face reflected in water, not wanting to be seen, much less recognized as he conveys himself to the far end of the school field. Standing sentinel along the perimeter fence, partially hidden, but by no means invisible in a windbreak of trees.

Within seconds he is approached by a small band of adolescents, singling him out by his incongruous style; white track shoes, straight-legged jeans, yellow UNLV sweater and Orlando Magic starter jacket. Not just excessively dressed, but palpably uncomfortable, if not to himself, then to anyone who can see him; a man who is not only unaware of how out of date his clothes are, but of how he feels with them on, perspiring for a number of reasons not all of them heat related.

"Hey Curbie. Gotta smoke?" says a boy, standing out from the group.

"Yeah, how many you want?" sez Curt.

"Six."

"Three dollars."

The kid collects fifty cents from each of his friends and hands it over to Curt who takes the money first then deposits the cigarettes in the kid's free hand.

"Got any weed, Curb?" asks another of the boys.

"*Noooo*. I don't sell drugs."

"You know you can make a lot more money selling dope than these."

"But it's illegal."

"So is selling cigarettes to minors."

"Barely."

The kid snickers to his friends as they walk away.

Curt watches the little ones gathered in clusters playing games, breaking off from the group to chase one other, trampling white clover blossoms and tumbling in the soft grass. He might be a man out for a walk, a delivery person, somebody's dad, but to eager eyes seeking their afternoon fix he is almost sure to have an extra cigarette, especially if they know him as Curt, Curbie, or hurtin' Curt.

He moves on to four more points of sale during the remainder of the 45-minute break. He'll be back after school and later on in the park.

On Fridays he visits the high schools and alternates between middle schools the rest of the week. Spending his free time at the zoo, mainly outside the primate grove, home to a family of mountain gorillas fathered and lorded over by 'Max' the silverback, who has been with the zoo since Curt was a child. Max is not territorial with Curt. He tolerates him as a stranger in a strange land, two hominoids diverged along evolutionary lines. One with a clutch of bananas, the other with his cigarettes, BigMac™, fries and shake, each searching the other's souls and smells for signs of kinship.

Curt does a cursory sweep of the ungulate enclosure; antelope, dik-dik, zebra, water buffalo, passing the falcon cage, snow leopard and beaver dam with barely a glance, as he makes his way towards his rendezvous with the balloon man.

He's there on the corner in his usual spot.

Curt runs up a little agitated. He knows what he wants this time.

Apart from their colour, the balloons are divided into two categories: translucent and solid, which have something to do with the meaning and significance of the balloon. The solid ones are more straight forward and can be summed up in a word or two; health, sex, money, power, new car, good job... things like that. The translucent ones have more subtle and complex meanings and usually come with morals or koans.

This time Curt is looking for a money balloon, something that will bring him more of that in his life. Although, as it is said, *you don't find the balloon, it finds you*, Curt feels it is he who seeks out the balloons on these days. Days when he feels close to meaning, as if it were less than a millimeter away; on the other side of a thin membrane.

Today there are white, yellow, orange and a kind of turquoisey blue; colours that wouldn't be out of place at a car dealership or corporate event, advertising neutrality, professionalism, function over form.

"What do you have?" says Curt.

The Balloon man knows that this isn't a question directed at him, he is merely the intermediary, giving his customers what is already theirs by right. "There's the balloon of *second chance*, the turquoise one there beside you, the balloon of *pray tell*, yellow, that's a truth one. I have another kind of truth one too, the white one over there, it's for giving away, you want one for you?"

"Yes."

"I think the best you could do is orange…"

"Ugh."

"What's wrong?"

"I don't like orange."

"I had more earlier; red and indigo, but those were clearly meant for someone else. I'm surprised this one is left. I think it's a sign. People very rarely get balloons that aren't meant for them. They'll sit here unbought until the right person comes along. It's a very good one symbolizing diplomacy in the way of influencing outcomes. It's lucky that you came by when you did."

"The green one's no good?"

"It's just for a reciprocal favour, it's also a giving one, you give it and you get something back, or you give it because you've received something from somebody."

"What about *second chances*?"

"Sure, go ahead, but it's only good for the rest of the day. I'd suggest getting one like this in the morning when it's more likely that you'll have a chance to use it. You'd better hurry up though. It looks like we have another customer."

A little girl rolls up on her bike avidly eyeing the balloons. Curt goes a little red, the pressure of making a decision weighing heavily on him now. He jerks his arm out toward the orange one mouthing the word and making the sound '...nge'.

"Good choice. I hope it works out,' handing it to him by its long jute string. "Don't let it go. Birds eat them and sometimes die. I'd feel bad if that happened. I have to guarantee my balloons, that also means getting them where they need to go."

"You make all these balloons yourself?"

"No, they're made by another person, or rather they're just made."

"How many are there?"

"Only as many as will sell at a time. They're like jobs, a job doesn't just disappear because no one does it."

"I don't have a job."

"Perhaps that's not the right analogy, you might think of them more as opportunities instead, like a *second chance* or an opinion, everyone's got one of those, but they're very subjective, that's why a balloon that's right for you won't go to someone else."

"I don't believe in opportunities."

"Perhaps you could just use some luck."

"Yes, yes, that's sorta what I was looking for."

"Come back tomorrow. I'm sure I'll have something. Just think very hard when you go home tonight and ask for some guidance. That's how this one works. The thought will turn into an intention and become a..."

"Okay, okay. I get it," Curt says, turning in the direction of home.

The little girl rushes forward, already pointing at the white balloon.

"Is this one for you?"

"*Yes.*"

"Well, may I suggest the turquoise one. It's good for a *second chance*, you may need one if you've been in any trouble lately or are planning to do so."

"Ohhh, well, it's pretty too, but I like white."

The only problem with the Balloon Man's prophecies is that they're almost always good. No one wants to buy a balloon that's going to make them unhappy, but the Balloon Man is your friend and he'll tell you the truth, even if it's hard. Every day he goes to his supplier and selects from the balloons that have sprung up overnight; just enough for that day and no more. The people who buy them are usually in a good mood already or are going to give them to somebody, which will put them in a good mood, the recipient or the giver, or both, so his news is generally positive, the red ones can be tricky though.

Once in his possession, Curt wastes no time in getting his balloon home. A lot can happen between acquiring your balloon and getting it to where you need to go. People with balloons behave much like those in the possession of illegal or potentially harmful substances. Furtively inhaling their contents in bushes, parking lots, alleyways, gas station toilets.

Sometimes he gets drunk, but it interferes with the balloon's efficacy. Set and setting are essential, as is one's state of mind. This is not something to be snorted or inhaled in some alleyway. Which is probably why they hadn't worked before. He needs to slow down. Make an intention, and visualize. Taking a deep breath, and letting it out before inhaling the contents of the balloon.

The Meaning of Orange

Curt likes to pair the intention with a number. He has great faith in the power of numbers, much more than words. He has a specific one in mind: 120,000; the number of hairs on the average human head. A number has to have significance, something that is important to him. He doesn't know many other numbers with special meanings, none higher at least. There are numbers that are lower, but not a lot that are higher. Millions and billions; the number of stars in the galaxy, the number of galaxies in the universe, have no significance for him. These, for the most part, represent things that he cannot see. He lives in a world of physical objects, things that he can buy, sell, find and lose; if it weren't for these things, he wouldn't know where he is, where he belongs. No, one hundred and twenty thousand is a good number.

He sits and breathes for a minute, thoughtfully running his fingers through his hair, imagining that he were coming closer and closer to this figure with every pass of his hand.

Diamond Reunion (After Midnight)

Lights flash in time with an adagio waltz. Mabel enters, all ribbons and bows, a version, or a vision of herself. Ron smiles as she makes her way toward him. They embrace and begin to sway a bolero, standing stiff and straight, gently pushing each other forward and back. Just like old times, or all times.

The others, Mickey, Doris, Martha, Linda, Maureen, Bernadette and Roy have come early, joined now by a new group.

"Hey, Tom."

"Hey, Linda."

"Where's that Lyle?"

"I haven't seen him."

"What about George? Where's George?" says Dorry.

"I saw him over there," pointing to a man in fedora and shirtsleeves.

"Who's that floozie with my George?" says Dorry, stomping her feet, but not to the music.

"I don't think she's from around here."

"She's that new girl, they call her Cleo, or Chloe or something," says Martha.

The music shifts into an upbeat swing, Glenn Miller, 'In The Mood,' 1944.

"I never used to get this pooped out doing the foxtrot," says Martha a little out of breath.

"Who's the band?"

"I don't see one."

"It's canned music."

"I used to be a ducky shincracker, now I got a bum knee," says Martha, bending over to inspect her leg.

"Quit your gammin' *giiiirl* I know a shincracker when I see one, and you ain't it," Linda, doing her best rendition of the twist.

"Are you kidding, that's not my Georgie, that's some old fuddy-duddy," says Dorry.

The music settles into a slow waltz.

"Hey, who dropped the beat?"

"I don't *feeeeel* well," says Linda.

Mickey smiles, "somebody spiked the punch with cough syrup."

"How can you tell?"

"Because it was me."

"Where's Georgie?"

"Right here doll."

"No. Noooo! You're too *ooooold*!"

"Well, so are you."

"Oh Frank, when are we going to blow this popsicle stand?" Maureen says, tugging at Roy's sleeve.

"I'm Roy, dear. Frank was your first husband."

"But, we… since when?"

There's an incident beside the punchbowl. Someone got punched. Drunk.

"Keep your hands offa her, *anchor clanker*," says Tom, brandishing a left hook.

"I was never in the navy," says Harold.

"Well, then you're either a coward or a commie."

"Neither, just a regular G.I. but I knew a lot a them Ruskies over there and they weren't half bad. Couldn't've done it without 'em."

"He still thinks he's on active duty," says Doris.

"Well, I'm about to give him The Broderick if he keeps it up."

"Break it up," says Betty "it wasn't Harold's fault, Ber is a share crop."

The members of the other group now begin to make their presence known, not exactly turned out for the occasion. One could say not appropriate at all. Dressed in solid colours, the same on the bottom as on the top, like pajamas. The men in camp-collars, like aloha shirts, but without the patterned prints, the women in V-neck tunics and loose-fitting, but snug pants of some thin, durable material.

"Well now, what do we have here?" says Doris, ready for a fight.

"I think they're from the other school."

"The other side of town."

"They're not very hep."

"Let's see what they got," says Ber jitterbugging onto the floor, shooting the girls on the other side of the room a devastating stare.

A tall man in camp-collars breaks ranks and approaches them.

"Who does he think he is?"

"He's cuttin' in."

"Oh no, he don't," says Tom.

"Guys, guys, I just have to check on Bill. He's asleep in his chair," says Camp Collars.

"Don't get fresh with me, I've got a steady fella and he'll whoop into ya'. He was a sergeant," says Ber.

"Still am," says Tom, looking as tough as he can with his cane.

"What... are you guys talking about?" says a young woman in yellow pajamas.

"And who are you, young lady? Isn't it past your bedtime?" says Doris.

"That's why we're here. It's almost 12:00."

"Twelve o'clock, well I'll... When..." Doris slips a little to the side, losing her grip on the walker.

The woman in yellow scrambles to help the older lady, "Mrs. Gables, are you alright?"

"Just give her a little time, she'll calm down. Offer her some tea."

"Would you like some tea?" says the woman in the yellow pajamas.

"I think I need some bennies. *Hey-ho*, does anyone have any bennies?"

"Is there a doctor in the house, my friend took a fall," says Tom.

Diamond Reunion (After Midnight)

The man in the camp-collars rushes over, "someone call an ambulance."

"Frank, are you alright, *oooooh*," says Maureen.

The music steadily creeps into the latter decades of the previous century, now playing Ray Charles' 'You Don't Know Me', 1962.

"What's this, I don't recognize this," says Doris, regaining herself.

"Do you like it?" says the camp-collar man maintaining an atmosphere of calm.

"Well, it's kind of slow. I prefer Glenn Miller or Guy Lombardo and His Royal Canadians."

"Sorry, I... I've never heard of that."

The ambulance attendants wheel in a gurney and wheel out a prostrated Roy.

"Ohhh, where's Frank?" says Maureen, more like a statement than a question.

"Who's Frank? I thought you were with Roy."

"Roy was my first husband, then Frank and now... now I'm all alone."

"He had to go to the hospital," says Camp Collars.

Martha emerges from the lavatory, dishevelled and screaming "She's ruining my *liiiiife*."

Mickey runs after, pants undone and red in the face.

"Hey, isn't that... the *ladies* room?"

"And who's that in there with them?"

"It's that new girl, I think her name is Cleo or Chloe."

Harold falls back, but lands in a chair which just so happens to have wheels, "well, that's all reet, I can still do the *do-si-do*."

The music changes again to 'I Want to Know What Love Is,' Foreigner, 1984.

"We have to go now Mrs. Gables."

"But, I haven't danced with Georgie yet," says Doris.

"Georgie's in bed, dear," says the man with the camp-collars.

"What time is it?"

"11:57."

"At night?"

"Yes, at night."

"*Oooooh, oooo-ooooh.*"

"What?"

"That's when… that's when Cinderella and her fella went a touralour alluring."

The room is nearly empty except for a few of the couples, the nurse in green and the man with the camp-collar.

"That's a pretty plain shirt to be wearing to a place like this. No one's gonna want to dance with you, unless you're with her," Doris jerking her head towards the nurse. "She's a plain Jane, you two were made for each other…"

The man in the camp-collars smiles at the nurse, now coming to assist.

"Wait a minute. Was I in a fight? How awful, and it was going so well until *your* lot showed up and took Georgie, you're a nice man though, aren't you?"

"Of course, I'm just here to help."

"Happy New Year!" says the nurse in green.

Muffled voices boom out 'Happy New Year!'

Sounds of fireworks crackle and spark through the speakers.

"Happy New Year," Mrs. Gables.

"Oh, you're *kidding.* What time is it?"

"12:00 on the dot."

"Oh no, I have to get to the ball, or I'll lose him *forever*!"

The music starts up again with 'Uptown Funk,' Mark Ronson, 2014.

Lights continue flashing through the darkened room, reflecting off streamers, confetti, foil wrappers, little pieces of plastic, a shattered pair of glasses.

"Whose are these?" says yellow pajamas, holding up the empty frames.

"Could be anyone's, they sometimes use the same prescription for different people," says camp-collars.

"I'll take Harold if you take Tom," says the green nurse.

"Be careful, they might start fighting again, I'd suggest a few milligrams of diazepam."

The nurse opens a sealed package of pills and takes out two white wafers, "time for the midnight special."

The boys open their mouths obligingly.

"Don't turn the lights on yet, wait 'til they settle down."

Tom maneuvers himself into the conveyance, too tired to speak.

The yellow nurse wheels him to his room, followed by the green nurse with Harold.

"Did I make it?" says Mrs. Gables, fading.

"You made it."

"And my shoes."

"Look," says the man with the collars.

"Oh, so shiny. I don't have to go back now. I can stay with you forever."

The nurse in green returns with an empty chair. Together they load her up and wheel her down the hall.

"What's that Mrs. Gables?" says the nurse.

She makes a faint mumbling sound, "*Ooooh,* Georgie. I don't have to go back. I never have to go back."

The Cloud Menace

There are two kinds of clouds on the horizon: Heaped white cumulus and dark, grey nimbus. Wads of fur caught in the tops of trees. Sheep or fluffy white Persians. Descending as if to land; a traveler in need of a break, merging with vinyl siding and shingled rooftops stacked up like frames in a film to walk on, to walk across water.

Thunder rolls over land, breaking up the thick cloudbank, scattering it eastward. One ahead of the others; a single cumulus separated from the woolpack peeking just over the top of that mountain there. Damp musky fur matted with dirt, seeking passage through blue sky pastures. Impressing those below with his artistic abilities, appearing in various forms; scaphoid (boat-like), Ansate (cup with handle), pyriform (pear-shaped), fungiform (mushroom-domed).

Aha! he thinks. *I'm the only cloud in the sky today. The world is mine.*

The purpose of most clouds is to ensure that the crops will grow, but this one acts alone. Stepping out in confident prospect of the day. Rain the furthest thing from its mind.

What harm can a little cloud do? you ask. But don't be fooled by his size. He's been hanging around the foulest water, relaxing in tailing ponds, stagnant pools, polluted lakes. Absorbing chemicals, bacteria, small animals, insects, sorting them like with like and dumping them farther inland.

He hovers on the perimeter of the storm, an almost solid object, like a thousand ghosts could converge on this point, hide a flying saucer in a bowl of soup, abduct a flock of geese or a whole football team. Stalking people through the streets, like it's only raining where they are. Humidity fogging glasses, flattening hair, smearing makeup, making one look shrewd irreconcilably, irretrievably lost.

Streetlights shine down on wet streets. Bringing out stains in the concrete, redolent of the effluvia of legions. Reflecting social glare in the crowds, solar glare in the clouds.

Pedestrians cower under hoods and awnings as he rushes up behind them, prompting a slip in the mud, wind up a dress, washing out roads, toppling trees, giving an unfair advantage to the rugby team.

Just bad luck they say, *it's only natural. As capricious as the weather.* Which makes him even more exultant as he flies over restricted airspace, through space fence, antennae array, breaking up momentarily in the wave guides, before coming back together on the other side.

His only natural enemy is the orgone man. Aiming his orgone gun and funneling the 'orgone' down through a pipe into a large metal tank.

The orgone man travels frequently, and far, picking the lonely clouds for his experiments.

People pay big money for the clouds, hoping that they will make them feel better, freer, happier, more in touch with the world.

He never knows when he might be pulled down and crammed into one of those metal tanks.

He almost was once, while he was in the shape of a lion. Feeling a drag, like a strong downburst and was barely able to escape. Banking sharply upward and doing an aileron twist, like a loop-de-loop, tearing part of himself away, but managing to save the rest.

The orgone man waits in position, aiming his gun at a spot in the sky, drawing down his orgone through a tube at the end of the pipe.

He spots the cloud, just cresting the top of a mountain and repositions his gun, aiming now for the little tuft of cumulus. The tuft rolls and pitches, but the orgone man is locked on, drawing down drop after drop, until it is a steady stream, filling the tank at his feet. Gradually the tuft disappears, leaving only the clear blue sky.

The orgone man gathers up the tank and loads it onto a cart that he pulls with the help of a dappled Andalusian. The cloud bangs and hammers against the sides of the tank, but the pressure keeps him in. Soon he will be taken to the Billionaire's enclave where he will be bathed in, consumed and eventually drained.

All his travels, exploits and memories absorbed by the Billionaire and his friends like so much wine, but unlike wine, they cannot simply wait it out. It will remain, like a dark cloud overhead. Following them wherever they go.

They will seek councilors, psychiatrists, therapists. They will try different forms of yoga, pilates, aerobics, tai chi. They will travel to various tropical locales, trying to leave the cloud behind, becoming old men, still searching for that thing that will let them forget, to float free of their bodies, to be at one with the clouds.

Rolando Orlando: Spectral Analyst

He's had a lot of near misses including a few movies, but nothing as memorable as the bespectacled host of the daytime show on KPAX. You see a little picture of him in the bottom corner of the screen with salt and pepper hair, black-rimmed specs, bowtie and blazer, always white, always sporting a polo in one, often many, neon shades.

Known variously as Rolando Orlando, Roland Oh Lando, Rollo 'roll the dice' or simply 'O'.

Spends most of his time at the beach, following waves up and down the shore; fractal coastlines communicating a little of the larger body of which they are a part. He sees patterns, but cannot read what they say. Scribbles on a sheet of paper scrawling to the horizon and back. A distance in time equal to a distance in space. Like the light that reaches his eye, already hundreds of thousands of years old. If only he knew what it meant.

He did two tours in 'Nam, during the second, he was bitten by a malaria-infected mosquito and ended up in a coma for nearly a week, when he emerged he could hear voices and read thoughts, which earned him an early discharge with a disability pension and a section 8.

Roland 'O' Orlando spectral analyst, hair almost completely white, tanned face etched with wrinkles as if he'd been pondering a slow thought all his life.

I need your help

The voice coming from somewhere behind.

"Hello?" turning around.

I'm right here.

Still looking in that direction.

Sorry... You can't see me. That's why I need your help. I'm kinda stuck here.

"Not now, can you come back later?'

When?

"Around 3:00."

The beach is both the beginning of the world and the end of it, as it was for the dinosaurs when the gulf of Mexico was hammered out by the massive comet that hit the Earth 65 (or so) million years ago, rising and sinking and rising again into the landmass known as 'Mu', Lemuria i.e. Atlantis, before it sank as well.

Rolando Orlando: Spectral Analyst

The dolphins tell him this, when they aren't in a trickster mood. There are two groups; Belial and Amelius B and A, A and B, who knows which is which.

Back when he had a talk show, some of the guests would claim that they were ghosts, after a while the furniture in the studio started showing up in unusual places and in unusual positions, there were a lot of lost lunches, bad smells, problems with the air-conditioning and frequent fire alarms.

One of his guests was a man who never lost his imaginary friend. The friend was also on the show and by all accounts did pretty well.

He was eventually fired for channeling a Russian dock worker with a very extensive vocabulary for anti-semitic speech.

A month later he got a job at the Seaquarium out on the Virginia Key, where he started petitioning to have all their Cetacea released.

"Can you explain this," says the director, holding out a pamphlet with Cetacean Revolution scrolled across the front and a picture of a whale capsizing a boat.

"It's an initiative for the repatriation of all sentient aquatic creatures as non-human persons," says Rolando.

"Do you realize that if we release these whales they will die, or be killed by other whales? You wouldn't be doing them a favour."

"They asked me to do it, they said they had a purpose for me, as part of their *Plan*."

"Why are you telling me this, if *I'm* their enemy?"

"They don't believe in dissembling. They want to be as honest about their plans as possible. Truth is the only communication."

Now he runs a counselling and animal rehabilitation group without a license right there on the beach. Attracting a fringe crowd of hippies and stoners on a quest to reconnect with the ocean; the home of all life on Earth and to which all life must return. Life comes second to the beach. Or rather, Life *is* Beach. And while certain beaches are known for certain things, the thing that all beaches have in common is the white sport coat guys. Different but the same, like Kens for whom Beach is both a lifestyle and a vocation.

They seem to have been there longer than anyone else, even before it was made popular by the syndicated television show.

Nearly everyone, aside from the ladies, wears at least one article of clothing from the show whether the white sport coat with the sleeves rolled up, the RayBan Wayfarers, the polos in every pastel shade imaginable or the white espadrilles, socks optional, but encouraged.

The population of these roving beach types is kept in balance by a private army of trend busters (former cool hunters) tasked with defending the character of the OG Old Guard elite MVIP (Miami Vice Intellectual Property Rights). Restricting any and all use of their likeness, including several attempts at a reboot. Citing all manner of indefensible legal grounds, which are largely ignored, especially since many of the offenders don't even know they're doing it.

Rolando is on the beach, hair slicked back, wearing

a white sport coat with a pink 'Florida' t-shirt. Sleeves still rolled up after eating a hamburger.

Another guy in the same outfit strolls up to him on the boardwalk and punches him in the face, "you look a little too much like someone I know," he sez, and keeps walking.

This happens all over town. Is it the 'Geraldo' hair and mustache, the pink shirt, the white sport coat with the sleeves rolled up? He owns three of the same jacket and a selection of t-shirts in multiple neon shades.

A couple of guys in black suits watch him as he runs back to his car, holding his nose which is now bleeding all over the coat. They follow him down Collins and onto the causeway. He does a fast maneuver, cutting through traffic to get into the left lane and takes the exit onto I-95, getting lost somewhere around the hospital, but it seems to work.

As soon as he gets home, he grabs all his white suits and neon polos and drives them as far out of town as possible, dumping them beside some garbage cans where someone less fortunate will surely happen upon them.

On the way back he picks up some western-style button downs, chinos and converse high tops. He catches a glimpse of himself in a shop window and has to look again to realize it's him. He could pass for just about anyone west of Houston, but out here at the beach he feels like he's from another planet.

"O'rlando!"

He pivots on the ball of one foot and goes down in a crouch, scanning his surroundings.

Again, "O-o'rlando!"

It *could* just be a coincidence, but then he sees a man approach, vaguely familiar.

"Hey, you still do surveillance?"

"*Shhhhh*, keep it down."

"I got this thing that needs looking into."

"What kind of thing?"

"I'm being followed."

"What? Now?"

"No, I lost 'em, but they know my routine and they're not subtle about it either."

"What do they look like?"

"Uh, tall, no distinguishing features. Black sunglasses, black suit and tie, driving an older model Oldsmobile."

"You better get a new style. You can't be walking around like that anymore. It's time to try something else."

"But this *is* my style."

"It doesn't matter. I had to get rid of my jacket along with all my other ones and my shoes."

"*Ohhhhh*, that's what's going on. I thought you were in disguise."

"I am, and you should be too."

"So that's it? You're not going to help?"

"I can give you my shirt if you want."

"Uh, no. I don't think it would fit."

"Suit yourself, don't say I didn't warn you."

He's the Geraldo Rivera of the paranormal. Was abducted by aliens once, but lies and says it is more. He does other people's shows now, but they're called 'podcasts'.

The listeners heckle him in the live feed.

"Ok, Ok, Seriously though, this one's true, I'm not making this up... sixxxxty-five percent of it is true... I was sitting in my car one day, when..."

The host rotates his hand to indicate 'keep it going...'

"And so, I was stuck there on the road and everything started to get brighter and brighter and I sort of felt myself float up into the air, then all of a sudden it was four hours later. I could tell because the time on the dashboard said 4:23. I don't know what happened to my watch, they must have taken it. It was a replica anyway."

During the break Rolando and the host have a private discussion with their mics turned off.

"What happened?"

"With what? The abduction or the watch, or..."

"With the story, you've got to keep it engaging, you can't have those long pauses."

"I find it hard to fill time, I need someone to bounce stuff off of until I get abducted again, I always come back with a bunch of new ideas."

"Just finish the interview. Or I'll make sure you really *do* get abducted."

He can't summon the dead on command, but he's pretty good at faking it. He's Rollo 'roll the dice' for a reason after all...

"Is there anybody here? Anyone at all?" He waits a beat, "*yes*, yes, I hear you. What do you want to say... okay, I will. He says he knows who the Zodiac Killer is."

"Is? You mean *was*."

"Yes," digging himself deeper. "His name is Walter Knight."

"Who's that?"

"That's his name... A-and he knows what happened to Malaysian Airlines flight MH 3-7-0."

"I thought part of it had been found."

"Nothing has been confirmed."

"What does he say about that?"

"It went down in the South Pacific Triangle. Like the Bermuda Triangle, but on the opposite side of the world. Antipodal. So like, things that fall into one side end up on the other, and vice versa."

"So, MH 3-7-0 is in..."

"The Bermuda Triangle."

"and Amelia Ehrhart is in..."

"The South Pacific."

The show cuts to a commercial.

An assistant unhooks his microphone, while another touches up his makeup.

"That was good, I think they bought it," says the host.

"If this is a podcast... then why is she doing my makeup?" Rolando asks of the girl.

"You have a face for radio... besides, there's a TeeVee studio in the building and our policy is to put makeup on everyone."

Rolando gets up to leave.

"The guy at the front desk will have your check," says the host, chewing on a Twizzlers.

They're waiting for him when he gets there.

"You have something that belongs to us," says the agent escorting him out of the building.

"Hey, who did you guys say you were with?"

"Nobody asked you," says the other one, opening the door of the Oldsmobile.

Rolando braces himself against the door frame, "Oh, come on. I did what you wanted, see?" giving them a full view of the western shirt and cut-off jeans.

"Get in," says the second agent, shoving him inside.

Rolando tries to scream, but they're already in motion, "I don't have *anything*."

"You are in possession of a videotape," says the first agent.

"What videotape?"

The second agent makes a face like, don't mess with us.

"A videotape of an object, you know... unidentified."

"Yes, yes I am. I did. I mean, I made it."

"You will give it to us."

They drive to his apartment without asking where it is.

Inside they do an obligatory tossing of his place before asking, "where's the tape?"

"It's in the drawer," pointing to the TeeVee stand.

He has a few different ones, all with corresponding dates.

"And the copies."

"I didn't make any copies, I really didn't."

They take all the tapes as well as the TeeVee and VCR.

"Hey, you don't need to do that."

"Yes. We *do* and you better be prepared to do what we tell you next time," says the first agent.

"Like what? Why don't you tell me now?"

"Like you make more of these tapes and maybe you keep living your life as usual. Maybe you even get to wear those suits again," says agent number two.

"Really?"

"We'll see."

He lays down on the bed, staring at the wall where the TeeVee used to be, thinking about suits.

Famous Monsters

Episode 1

Secondhand sun falls through glass, casting exaggerated shadows on stone walls; two-dimensional demons eeking out their short ephemeral lives on the periphery. Taking up residence, or residue there in the cracks and fissures. Too thick to slip back through before dawn.

Storm clouds hover between twin empyreans of Los Angeles and the Milky Way.

The famous actor picks up the receiving end of the princess phone and dials.

A sultry feminine voice hums over the line, "hello Christopher."

"Are we still on for dinner?"

"Yes, of course. I've been waiting for you."

"I will be leaving soon, is there anything I should bring."

"I want to see our baby."

"Baby? *Oh yes...* the baby," says Chris, hanging up the phone, "Benjamin."

A small feeble hunchback enters from the passage, "Yessir?"

"Bring the car around, we'll be leaving to pick up Miss Stephanie."

Christopher waits for Benjamin to recede before exiting by a separate route. His footsteps are the only sound as he makes his way down a dimly lit hall to a small room made up to look like a child's bedroom. No specific gender or age. He does a brief turn of bewilderment like he's in the wrong place, then with a flourish, picks a doll up off the floor and carries it with him to the car.

8:30 pm.

A black stretch limo rolls into the manicured driveway of Stephanie St. Marie, the beautiful and successful glamour actress, Chistopher's love interest and leading lady.

She appears in the doorway of her palatial home big with child and brandishing an umbrella to shield her piled coiffure from a light pattering of rain. Bats swarm overhead as she is whisked into the car by Benjamin.

"Good evening dear," says Christopher richly.

They exchange pecks on the cheek, no tongues until after dinner. He gives her the doll swaddled in its pink blankie.

"Our ba-by," cries Stephanie. "I can't wait to have a baby of our own, after all this time and the operation."

"A baby of our own," Christopher muses.

"What should we call it?"

"Oh well," he's got a few ideas, but blurts out, "Robert seems appropriate, or Roberta."

Stephanie shrinks in her seat.

"Or, perhaps Madelleine."

"Ugh, Christopher, this is not the 19th century."

"Oh, I keep forgetting that..."

The restaurant is on the ground floor of a private club/ hotel teetering on the edge of the canyon.

"Oh, Christopher, don't you *ever* look in the mirror. Your hair is a mess and you have, what is this? Blood on your face?"

"No, um, it's tomato juice. I'm trying to increase my stamina, for when the baby comes."

"Oh, I'm so happy you are thinking of our future."

A silent old man attending the door takes their coats. Organ music plays as they enter. Candlelight flickering across yellowed wallpaper.

A waiter, looking like a thousand-year-old vampire brings a bottle of Chateau Briand on ice and retreats into the copperish glow of the room.

Christopher takes a sip and places the glass down slowly, parting his lips for words when he is interrupted by a clipped voice and bright light.

"CUT. That was great you guys," says a man in crewcut and horn-rims. "Frank could I ask for a little more blood on your fangs when you're taking their order, and Christopher, can you kick it up a notch? I want them to be scared *just by the sight of you.*"

"Can do."

"What about me?" says Stephanie, gazing at her reflection in a polished spoon.

"You look lovely," replies the director.

"Christopher?"

"Beautiful darling," he says, sheepishly.

"Ok everyone, take your places in three, two, one, action."

"Ooh, Christopher dah-ling, when are we going to get mar-ried? I can hardly wait for you to take me to the Bahamas for our *ho*-on-ey *mo*-on," managing to make both o's into *oo*'s.

"Soon my dear, soon. I have work to do before I can commit my time to anything else."

"Even me?"

"I'm afraid so dear."

Stephanie attempts to weep like squeezing blood from a stone.

"Cut. *Stephanie*, what's the matter? This man has just rejected you, choosing his detestable work on mutants over you. How do you feel about that? You should be throwing water in his face. Gouging his eyes out with your dessert spoon and spitting into the bleeding sockets!"

"I, I, I. I can't," screams Stephanie in despair.

"Why? what's going on?"

"I, I, I. I'm pregnant," she cries into her napkin.

The cast and crew exhale and don't appear to breathe in.

Stephanie shudders with contractions as if the baby has become overly conscious of itself in the womb and is making an effort to escape.

Before anyone has a chance to move or even breathe, Christopher has Stephanie in his arms and is rushing her out into the night. Her screams audible long after they have disappeared.

An outbuilding appears further from the edge of the canyon than it should. Chris kicks the door open and lays Stephanie down on a narrow cot. No time to get comfortable before she goes into labour. A hairy head emerges, then two legs, two more legs and a short, curly tail. The monster shrieks in discomfort as Stephanie looks on in horror and passes out.

Christopher smiles, embracing the tiny freakish being; still what one might call cute, with its cleft upper lip exposing tiny useless fangs.

"My son! My son!"

The director enters, looking on in astonishment at the makeshift structure and bloody tableau on the bed, "What the hell have you done? You just cost me my cast and my movie. I'll never get off the ground for another film."

"Never mind that now, Horatio. Stephanie has just given birth to a most magnificent thing indeed."

Horatio looks at the child and the prone body of Stephanie, "what the hell kind of stunt is this? We're not even rolling tape. What is the meaning of this?"

"Breeding stock for my own… species." Out of breath from elation, "that will be called, *Christiphus Canidae.*"

Christopher wraps the wolverine baby in the blanket formerly occupied by the girl doll and tucks the whole thing into the loosened front of his cummerbund, "You must excuse me, I have somewhere I need to be." Chris exits through the roof, topcoat flapping like wings.

Horatio scoops Stephanie off the bed, barely making it out of the building before the floor gives way to darkness. He forges onward inventing a set that will carry them through to the next scene, tentatively feeling for ground that could give way at any moment. He's got to be out of his mind, walking into another man's imagination like that.

He keeps his eyes fixed on the light from the restaurant and doesn't avert his gaze until he's there, realizing only then that he is holding the inert body of Stephanie St. Marie.

They enter through a side door to find all but three of the crew, including various members of the cast, lying unconscious, some with eyes open, others closed.

Horatio packs what he can of the gear and calls for an ambulance, "do you have anything like a bus. I've got a cast and crew of 19 people all of whom have fallen into some sort of catatonic trance."

"Are you okay sir? Has there been an outbreak of some kind?"

"I think you could call it a mass psychosis followed by symptoms of emotional withdrawl."

"Are you certain?"

"Most certain, there was a traumatic incident that took place here not an hour ago that has left members of my company paralyzed. Are you going to send someone?"

"We'll have an ambulance there as soon as possible. What is your location?"

"An ambulance? I need about ten ambulances."

"How many people did you say there are?"

"Twenty... Hello?"

"I was just thinking... we can usually get more than one person per unit, sometimes three if they do not need to be prostrate."

"That's fine, we can prop them up, even a taxi, can you call one of those?"

"What is your location?"

Horatio gives them the address of the hotel/restaurant in Coldwater Canyon. From outside he can hear the ambulances winding up, converging from several points of origin; Cahuenga, Mulholland, as far south as Franklin and La Brea, a few of which seem to have gotten lost, or misdirected. When they arrive he explains to a scrum of paramedics, police and emergency workers the nature of the emergency, but aside from their prone, listless states nothing medical has occurred.

"Who's... in charge?" says one of the cops.

"That guy over there," says Horatio, pointing to a man in a canary suit, his head in the lap of another unconscious man, bent almost in half.

Paramedics load the crew onto gurneys and wheel them out like furniture.

Horatio is inspected by a small woman in blue scrubs. After the obligatory finger count and eyeball check he is allowed to leave. His car blocked in by just about every other car in the lot and a line of emergency vehicles, proceeding in a torturous circuit up the steep canyon roads. He begins his descent on foot, slipping down embankments and hillsides until he reaches Sunset, walking another ten blocks before he can find a cab that is willing to take him to Culver City.

He lays low for a few days, the network is anxious to keep the situation secret, but word has spread via friends and family of the crew. Horatio and the film studio scramble to put together a new cast. Most of Horatio's movies haven't yielded more than 100 thousand dollars, but that's still more than it cost to make them. His production company, *Horatio Richards Presents* went bankrupt last year and now the only way he can get anything made is by adhering to a strict set of conditions and deadlines.

Later in the week Horatio is having a conversation with Stanwick, the casting director about the project. "The ones that aren't in comas are emotional wrecks and won't leave their homes. I haven't seen or heard from Chris in a week. I'm starting to think something very strange is going on."

"Do you have anyone lined up for the pilot?"

"How? No one wants to work with me after what happened."

"W-well… if you don't get something together soon you're gonna lose the TV spot and probably most of the sponsors."

In a panic Horatio throws tapes and scripts around the office searching for his address book and keys then drives out to Chris's prefab castle built on a pile of rocks in Benedict Canyon. Through the gate he sees the yellow Mustang.

Horatio screams into the intercom, "Chris. I know you're in there. You better have something for me and good."

The gate swings open, Chris is waiting in the doorway dressed in a long white coat.

"What's this? You don't like bathrobes?"

"I was in the middle of something."

"Well so was I, until my lead actor took off into the night with a feral child under his arm."

"I am sorry for all of that, but it will all become clear once I show you what I have been working on."

Episode Two

Chris leads Horatio to a stairwell at the end of a long hall, passing through a door and onto an elevated walkway above what appears, on closer inspection to be an air raid shelter or bug out room. The motte part of the motte-and-bailey. Much larger and deeper than it looks from outside. There are large steel crates, tall enough to hold a prisoner, as well as a dentist's chair, an iron maiden and a medieval rack.

"Wow, this is amazing. This isn't what I was expecting at all. It's so realistic. We've really got somethin' here."

"I have this idea... 'The Last Movie Ever Made,' it writes itself. You follow me?"

"No, not really."

"Do you ever wonder why they keep making these stupid movies. We're going to give them one last *oomph*, huh?"

"You mean sell it to them?" says Horatio.

"Yeah."

"What if they don't buy it?"

"The way I planned it, they won't be able to refuse," Chris doesn't try to disguise a very devious smile indeed as he fiddles with some dials on a console.

"What's the story? Mad scientist unveils unbelievable new experiment. We need cameras. We need to document this. All we need now is a cast. People love to be in movies. We'll just conscript some random people. I know a few actors that'll do it. I'll be back in a couple hours with a cast and crew."

Chris is busy reading an ECG print out.

"Chris?"

"Absolutely, I agree. Go get the gear."

"Good, yeah prepare some genius experiments for us. This is great. I totally underestimated you, man. When were you gonna tell me about this anyway?" Horatio leaves the rhetorical question hovering in the dank basement as he ascends to the surface of mock-Hollywood-pirate-pilot-propaganda to further shred his reputation.

With little to offer in the form of recompense Horatio rounds up the required participants for a brief sight-reading of the script scribbled into the back of his day planner.

He works the bars of West Hollywood where the has-beens are known to hang out announcing that he needs extras *for a movie*. They're not a very motivated bunch, so he buys everybody a round, as well as food and booze for the set.

"This is ridiculous. I don't even know what it's about?"

"You're not supposed to. That's how you capture your true character and motivation."

"By having it largely unscripted?"

"Just act natural. You're an actor, right?"

"Mmmmhmm... Just give me a second," the actor waves his hands around in front of his face, smooths back his hair and clears his throat.

After assigning roles to each of the actors, Horatio carpools the cast of drunks and movie enthusiasts into one of Hollywood's most secluded lairs to perform a would-be mass slaughter of the innocent and not so innocents.

Episode Three

By turns the makeshift cast and crew gaze out at the opulent frontage of exclusive Hollywood homes and back at their reflections in the window. Unsure of whether to consider themselves tourists, or amoung those who rule and built this city. Only a matter of hours ago they were questioning whether they would ever make the ascent from the lowly haunts of Westchester, Compton and Inglewood, to the precipitous heights of Laurel or Coldwater Canyon to do anything other than look. But now that they have, they gaze back at the city with a kind of disdain, promising never to return, or at least, not completely.

The gate is open when they arrive. Horatio knocks on the door and waits a beat before entering.

"Chris, Chris! We're back... he must be downstairs," he says to the others.

The lights are off and its colder than it needs to be this time of year.

The few pieces of furniture there are have been ripped up; cushions torn, stuffing falling out in wet wads of mildewed fluff. The cast and crew remaining enthusiastic despite any kind of reception or pretext to their safety.

"He must have the air conditioning on," says Horatio. "Chris... We're coming down."

Still no answer.

"Start rolling film," says Horatio.

"There's no director?"

"I'm the director," says Horatio.

"What do you want us to do?"

"Just let the action point the way."

"What action?"

"Wow, this is so authentic, like the set of an old horror movie," says one of the actors.

"It even smells like a dirty, haunted house," says another.

Horatio leads them to the door at the end of the hallway and down the stairwell to the secret lair/ lab.

"Okay, get ready."

The camera's eyes lock onto the scene before them, steeped in the dramatic silence that fills a soundtrack as when the invader meets and assesses the incumbent lord's army.

"Ladies and gentlemen. Meet Christopher Marshall, the greatest actor, scientist and renaissance man of our time."

Chris stares at the group benignly, stretching the moment to the limit of rational human thought, hesitation, weakness, panic, to whatever lies beyond. Time slows down, no one speaks or moves. Gradually the sound of a flute becomes audible, rising to the pitch of an alarm. A figure lunges toward the group en masse, followed by two others; bipedal, with a mix of bear and canine features, moving as well on four legs as on two.

On the first pass, the rabble chews through the cast and crew, returning a second later to tear them limb from limb. Cameras roll towards the floor like heads away from their bodies. Horatio clamors for higher ground, observing from an overhang in the ceiling.

Chris joins in the carnage, blood dripping from his chin, "I respect you, Horatio. You are godfather to my child, Gruk Tin Bok."

"I don't wanna die. I just want to make a movie. Please. I just wanted to make a movie."

"We *are* making a movie. It just isn't the movie you thought it would be. *It's better.*" Chris continues as if to comfort his bewildered guest with a false sense of security. "Things happen that one could never plan or put on a stage. We are the lead actors in the play that is our life, *all the time*, not just during those few isolated scenes executed with sterile, immaculate precision. It's like a play set in a hospital. How *depressing...* Instead, I'm capturing all those moments together, releasing them, when the time is right, in one grand display.

This is only the *beginning*. The thing is, by the time it's finished, there may not be anyone left, to watch it."

Horatio makes his way towards an air-conditioning duct and climbs inside.

The creatures fight over the last few scraps while Chris whistles a jaunty tune.

"Horatio, Hor-a-t-i-o, come out, co-oome o-oout" singing along to the melody of his extemporized song. "There's only one way, the o-only way, for *both* of us."

The creatures go off in search of him, returning a few seconds later with a despondent Horatio, looking very much shrunken in size.

"Horatio? Are you in there," knocking on the top of his head. "did you pass out? Don't worry. My children are perfectly trained. They would not hurt you unless I told them to, and how much and for how long. C'mon, Horatio, come on and talk to me."

Horatio flinches, surfacing from his dissociative state, "d-don't, don't let them hurt me."

"They won't, they are really as kind as can be. It isn't like this where they come from. It's our world that is cruel, not them."

The monsters sigh and applaud the master.

Horatio averts his eyes, trying to wriggle out of his own body, as if he could make himself small enough to slip into another world.

"C'mon Horatio, we have places to be."

Chris snatches a hypodermic needle off of a tray. The monsters increase their grip until the only thing he can move is his head.

"You're going to make me miss that vein. You won't like it if I put it through your Adam's apple, it *stings*."

"Rrrrrahhh," Horatio yells and grits his teeth.

Chris hits the jugular despite Horatio's squirming and presses the plunger, "you can't fight it. It's Thorazine."

When he wakes up they are outside. It's colder, not as smoggy. In fact, he doesn't see the city at all. He pivots to the right, the beach is where it should be, the Canyons and the mountains behind, but everything else is flat. The neighborhoods of Covina, Huntington Park, Paramount all the way to Irvine are as one indistinguishable mass. He had never imagined it that way until now. The glint of the river flowing all the way to the Pacific, visible now without the heavy covering of smog.

He knows, but asks anyway, "where are we?"

"I wanted somewhere quiet to think…"

Horatio looks behind. All there is is a squat stone structure. Further up the shore he imagines he can see Santa Barbara and beyond it, Point Conception. It's an amazing feeling, like flying.

He doesn't want to betray himself, but can't help it, "how is this possible, how did we get here?"

"I wanted to make something of my own. This is merely a place to rest my eyes during the long journey, to Irokindo…"

The tableau disappears. They are back in the dank basement. Christopher removes a pair of goggles from Horatio's face and shows them to him, "the big data centers already have all the information in the world. They know what we like, don't like, watch, don't watch, but the mysteries of the mind, of the *preliterate* world, are still tightly locked up in here," tapping Horatio's skull, "and we can retrieve them."

"That was all... a simulation?"

"Arguably the whole world is. But there is a world *behind* the world and that's where the simulation begins... That's where we *change*... the *movie*. Eventually everyone is going to be wearing these things. It will replace life. So, it only makes sense. If people are going to be spending so much time there, we might as well get there first."

"It sounds like the end of the world," says Horatio.

"No, *Irokindo*, that's what I call it. It's so much easier to think of a place if it has a name."

"Stop, it doesn't have to be like this. We can work something out."

"What are you blubbering about, can't you see? I *am* doing this, and if I'm doing it, *you're* doing it. Think of it, like, we're partners."

"But if we're partners, I can say no."

"But I can insist, after all, you enabled me through your films; an empty bottom to siphon money into. No other studio would have let me do those things, thanks buddy. We make a good team."

"I didn't know what was happening. I thought it was for a movie. You've blown it all out of proportion."

"Well, how else would I be able to explain what I was up to. I had to work. I had to express myself, lay it all on the table for everyone to think it wasn't real when it *was*. You could say you had nothing to do with it, but it was your company and your name on the top of the page. You're the one they'll go after. You're my fall guy. You see how it works?"

Horatio looks ready to cave.

"I need you to work with me, like in the old days. You give me what I want, I give you what you want… Don't worry, you'll have some time to think about it. In the meantime…"

Chris picks up and blows into a tiny flute. "Gather round," he says, as if speaking to a group of children, but retaining his resonant and eerie gravitas.

The monsters rally around, swaying from side to side, anxiously awaiting their orders.

"Now you know what to do. Here," showing them some articles of clothing and whispering some subtle commands before unlocking and opening a heavy steel door.

The animals lurch forward into the cool night air. Their dirty feet coming clean in contact with the soft, green grass.

Horatio tugs on his restraints, screaming, "help, HELP," before Chris slides the door shut.

"The Olmec were the ancient precursor civilization to the Aztecs. They revered a werecougar baby mutation whose origin could only be explained by divination of the gods. They sacrificed people and ate of their flesh to gain spiritual insights and praise in the eyes of the maker. Life!" he shouts, "Can be mastered through sacrifice. To deny the force that takes us is to deny our own lives."

"So what, they're part of some genetic modification experiment gone wrong a few thousand years ago? Where have they been all this time?"

"That's just it, they haven't been anywhere. I had to bring them here."

"How?"

"By following the ancient rites of sacrifice."

Chris turns to a large metal case with a high steel door, "I have a few surprises for you yet, but first let me show you my greatest creation of them all. Behold." He pulls a red velvet cord. The door slides open.

"This is my son, Gruk Tin Bok, of course you met him briefly after that business at the restaurant" a furry toddler/ wolf/ cougar animal stands hunched forward, somewhat clumsily, but agile in a mutant-freak sort of way. Soft grumbling sounds percolate in the creature's throat. He has Chris's hair and a horrific mixture of animal and human features.

Chris softly pats the creature's head. A look of pride and loneliness crosses his face, "He is yet too young to go about his true calling. He must stay with me until he is older. Then he may go with the others." He pauses briefly in abeyance of an emotion, "I love these animals. They are, my family. I have given them life. They depend on me. They greet me with awe and reverence. I am all intelligence, beauty, trust and hope to these creatures. I am all... they have."

Horatio is exultant for a moment, coming out of his torpid gloom, "you're *dead*, aren't you?"

"Yes, I must consume the hepatic products of warm-blooded mammals as sustenance in order to maintain the basic biological functions of a sentient creature," pausing in a sort of rapture. "I apologize for the inflated language, but there is no direct way to explain how one can appear to be both dead *and* alive. I'mean I don't have any real autonomy, rather I'm compelled by the will and impulse of the darkness. I identify with the creatures of the night and become one of them, suffering insatiable hunger between meals."

Horatio notices for the first time a row of tanks lined up against the wall opposite. After a few seconds he recognizes forms, and then faces. They are *people,* suspended in an opaque viscous fluid. It's hard to imagine them as human and even harder to imagine them as humans he knows; Luke, Denise, Monica, One of the Baldwins, and other lesser known actors and actresses, not as readily identifiable by their first names.

"Yes, they are here with us as well. It was hard to get them, but with a little help we might look forward to a more succulent occasion…"

"What?"

"I always wanted to say that."

Horatio looks confused.

"Don't worry, it's a reference, soon though we will have more and our movie will be ready."

"What do you do with them?"

"I upload them into the mainframe of this computer," tapping a metal box, "while their bodies are held in suspended animation."

Horatio looks as if that wasn't the question he was asking, "but how?"

"I enlisted the help of some scientists, little did they know that they would become part of the experiment themselves. AI is the future, and now what we have is a movie-making machine. Don't worry, you will see soon enough."

Horatio hears the words but doesn't comprehend. His attention is drawn elsewhere, "what's that?"

"CCTV from the corner of Hollywood and Vine," says Chris of a screen on the wall, "and that's a live feed from the cameras I've secured to the creatures' chests," of a monitor on the table. "By morning, this place we call *Los Angeles* will be, well, it won't have changed much at all, but we will be one step closer to our goal."

Episode Four

Howls and screams pierce the still intrigue of wee morning hours.

So and so and so and so are in front of Craig's on Melrose, smoking.

"Hey, is that a chupacabra?" without irony.

"What the… there's another one."

"It must be a shoot."

"But, I don't *see* any cameras."

"Or lights."

"Do they look like crew?" pointing to a group across the street.

"Jimmy, they all look like crew."

"The moon is full, maybe they're trying to get natural light."

"Do you still see them?" says Jimmy.

Nobody else seems to have noticed.

"Ahhhhhh."

"Was that… a scream?"

"It sounded pretty legit."

"Jimmy, hey whoa."

The creature leaps out and grabs Jimmy around the waist, "get him offa me."

"Hey, whoa! Somebody!"

Plenty of people are watching now.

"How is this real?" says a bystander.

"Did you see that?"

The monster disappears around the corner with 'Jimmy' tucked under its arm like a baby.

Chris watches the display with the elan of a sports fan rooting for the home team, tracking the chaos through the streets, beginning at Hollywood and La Brea and continuing west southwest to Sunset, Melrose then north onto Doheny and back up to Sunset.

"Who believes in monsters now? Huh-huh? You buffs!" Chris roars.

"How many of those things have you got?" says Horatio.

"You mean my *children*, well, actually only one of them is my child. The others were summoned through the sacrificial rites."

"Never mind."

"There are five, not counting young Gruk."

"So, what's the plan, you're not worried that they might get shot, or caught?"

"Absolutely not. They're not from this plain of existence. They do not by rights even exist at all. It is our belief, or rather our suspension of *disbelief* that creates them. And in a place like this, where almost everything is made up, they are quite a lot stronger."

If he weren't in such a compromised position, Horatio would be right on board with the idea. He would pitch it himself, but it is no longer an idea, it is no longer fiction, and he, with his preference for fantasy over reality, fiction over truth, had helped make it happen.

Episode Five

Inside the actor's studio with Christopher Marshall:

"The name of tonight's guest is synonymous with intrigue. He's appeared in films such as *Blue Velvet, Highlander, Death Proof, Willy's Wonderland* and plenty of others please welcome Christopher Marshall."

Marshall does his trademark wave and scary face "Boo."

The host plays along, cowering in mock horror.

"You know, as I was approaching the stage… I had the odd sensation, that *this* would be, an historic occasion," says Chris.

"Tell us, what are some of your latest projects?"

"Genetic engineering fascinates me, we're at the point now where we can create life and by the same token enable ourselves to live on indefinitely."

"And how does this fit into the plot?"

"Frankenstein was a mutant, but he was also a man."

"Horror movies, is that your new niche?"

"My favorite dreams are nightmares. I'd like to make a movie out of them, then watch the movie a thousand times to see how far down this rabbit hole, in my own head, really, goes."

"I'd pay to see what goes on in your head, Chris."

Chris laughs, "No. You wouldn't," he pauses, dropping the tonality of his voice. "Do you know what it is about acting? It's that feeling of tension in your spine. Doing the unpredictable that would give even your spirit a funny feeling, like, *isn't this strange?*" Chris leans over and whispers "The actor… is closest to himself, when he speaks… in a low tone and lets, the words, fall… within his own being. Both the audience, and the person to which he is communicating must be close, as close as his conscience, for the real creature, himself, to *break lose*," reaching out as if to grab James by the throat.

James flinches and takes a few shallow breaths allowing the tension to settle before resuming, "I'd like to ask you about your role in the new Robert Rodriguez adaptation of Dracula with yourself in the role of the count. You will have to fight such opponents as Jason Statham and Mark Wahlberg, it is also rumoured that Rosanna Arquette will be your concubine."

"Those are unfounded rumours and it would be unfortunate if they were true, since the theme of the story is young love, so a movie starring all old people would be, well, depressing. The fact is that no one has been cast for the roles. The script has only now been passed through the second draft and is being distributed to prospective actors and actresses before it is put through still more drafts."

"Is it normal for a script to go through so many drafts?"

"It is, but it is not often that a feature is produced based solely on the cast's suitability. Usually, the script will be adhered to as much as possible, but here we want to get the right people and adapt the story, accordingly."

"I understand George A. Romero has requested you for a part in *his* new movie as well."

"In dead, *a hem*" he coughs and clears his throat, "I mean, indeed he has James. I'm really excited about this project. In hopes that others... soon... will be, too."

"And you're getting married..."

Chris grips the arms of the chair, fighting an urge to run.

"It has been said that during the filming of your latest movie that..."

"*Ohhh, ohhh*, no. Here they come."

"That, there was an interruption."

Shadowy figures emerge from the corners and cracks in the wall, gathering a presence there in the room. Chris goes stiff in the chair, legs out straight, feet sliding across the floor "warriors… they're coming for me… sharp knives and spears…"

"Oh, I see, this is like a sneak peek."

"Don't come any closer, I'll show you where they are. I'll take you to them," Chris dodges a spear, rolls and runs off the set.

"Well, there he goes. Christopher Marshall, a fine, fine actor *indeed*."

The creatures return at first light bearing a selection of Hollywood celebs, exhausted and disheveled from trying to fight off their assailants.

"Have a seat," says Chris, as the creatures place them in restraints and carry them to a semi-circle of chairs bolted into the floor.

"It's you," says the actor with the dimpled grin and botox cheeks.

"You didn't think you'd see me again, eh? No longer running in the same circles, but our fates are intertwined."

"Let us go," says the famous actress.

"But you are my guests, aren't you curious what I have brought you here for?"

There are screams and frustrated outbursts lamenting the futility of the situation.

"No? Then may I direct your attention to the wall," pointing at the tanks.

"You mean… those are really?"

"You know who they are."

"Oh my god! Luke?"

"And soon you will be with them," says Chris, as each one is injected with the Thorazine.

He didn't get the fear he wanted out of these particular subjects, but he got what he needed. There is already a lot of pretty frightening things in there; even some real live deaths.

Horatio is slumped forward in the office chair, badly in need of a shower after soiling himself. Chris shoots him up with a combination of ketamine and Benzedrine and escorts him up a flight of stairs to the disinfection/ decompression chamber. The creatures strip him naked and push him through the door.

"Are you going to gas me? Go ahead, I don't care."

"No, no no. We need you *alive*. You are going in there," says Chris over loudspeakers mounted both inside and outside the chamber.

Adjacent to the chamber are the tanks, thirteen in total. Ten of which have already been filled. Horatio stands dispassionately in the chamber as he is sprayed down from a shower nozzle in the ceiling.

A warm breeze blows him dry after which a green light flashes, signaling him to exit the chamber.

"Get in the tank," says Chris.

Horatio doesn't move, "I'd rather die than entertain your depraved fantasies any longer. I'm not one of your creatures."

"We could live forever Horatio, anywhere, anytime."

"This is never going to work. There's always going to be death. You can't do anything about that."

"Sure, we'll get tired of it all, we'll die, but it'll be a choice when we do. I love life too much to waste it here. I used to think that I could win out over nature, but of course, I can't. So, I found a way around it. To survive into a truly new day. To witness a new era. Learning from our ancestors what they themselves told me on that fateful night in Mexico City."

"Well, that isn't the life for me. I don't care how bad it gets, or how pointless my life seems in the process. I am one more person that walked the earth, that contributed and anyone who leaves, or opts out, or doesn't participate, is a coward."

"Suit yourself."

Horatio makes a few feeble attempts to break through the shatterproof, hermetically sealed glass.

"It's just for a little while, in the meantime there will be plenty of things to keep your mind occupied in Irokindo. I have programmed every futuristic scenario I could think of. I have also arranged for us to be reintroduced to 'Earth' as soon as it reaches optimum conditions; that is of atmosphere, temperature and water. We wouldn't want to wake up just any olde time and expect it to be spring would we? Nope, no taking chances with these things, this is our life! Aye matey?"

Chris patiently waits for Horatio to crack, eating McDonald's happy meals with his rabble on a long, wide banquet table and singing lullabies.

"I admire your courage and moxy, Horatio. This experience of yours will do you good. The stubborn ones are always the strongest, and you take the cake."

Horatio goes from standing, to sitting to eventually lying down. Chris disrobes and dons a blue spacesuit before entering the chamber. Horatio doesn't move, flinching slightly at Chris's distant spacesuit touch as he is hoisted into the thick, rubbery goo, supporting him there for eternity.

Bobbing around in Christopher's program of the ultimate horror movie is a truly grisly affair. AI demons chase him down alleyways, through warehouses, apartment complexes, deserted big box stores. Silently looming on the peripheries before they burst out of the machine. At some point he realizes he's not alone. There are others, more than he can probably count, and they aren't having a good time. Celebrity or not, there is nothing fun or influential about being chased through the middle of nowhere by the contents of your own—and who knows how many other's—minds.

There are glimpses of movies, or what *could* be movies, given the company he has, but they are never the same for long and not being able to follow them is maddening. He can't even concentrate on his own thoughts. Slamming into walls in the middle of fields, holes in the street, doors that open into empty sky, windows onto underground tunnels. It becomes clear that there is no order to it. Whoever programmed it, either didn't know what they were doing, or died before they could finish. Even the reveals, when they are allowed to take place, are sort of an afterthought; badly drawn monsters living out their own lives in a two-demon-sional world. Done no justice, not allowed to do harm; first they must escape the program.

Chris is no artist; that's for sure. His hubris and lack of attention to detail have created monsters, indeed, but Horatio is everything he could ever want in a psychologically dependent captive; equal parts traumatized, desensitized and enthralled, but even Chris acknowledges the effects that this type of programming would have on a human mind.

There will be long troughs of soundless sleep, followed by peaks of mental and physical activity and mind-numbing daytime T.V. Everything you need for a fulfilling human existence.

Chris monitors his subject's biorhythms for a few hours before introducing himself into the system. The tank shudders with the release of the excess energy, turning the pinkish goo an even brighter pink. Chris' body arcs up and out then goes limp as the soul casts off its corporeal shell, supplying power to the machine as it is sucked into the mainframe.

Lights flicker on the console, a voice intones, "is everybody here?

Famous Monsters

Kidnapping Victims Rescued from Benedict Canyon Residence Yesterday Morning

The movie industry is reeling after the discovery of eight of its own in a Benedict Canyon residence yesterday morning.

Investigators were led to the house in Benedict Canyon after cellphone pings turned up in the neighborhood.

The persons were reported missing Tuesday, but the full scope of the investigation was not realized until early Friday morning.

Although there have been no reported deaths, all victims, including the perpetrator are in coma.

No details have been released into the cause or the possible mental or physical condition of the victims and no names have been released.

Daily Breeze, March 2, 2023

Hollywood Actors Kidnapped for Experiments by Movie Producer and Financier Christopher Marshall

The movie industry in Hollywood is under a new type of focus, as details of the inexplicable events at the home of Christopher Marshall begin to roll in.

So far none of the victims have died, but the mystery deepens as reports of a 'virtual studio' emerge. Anonymous sources have alleged that Marshall had been making 'virtual films' in the basement of his replica castle in Benedict Canyon. The exact nature of the films are still unknown, although sources say that they may have involved the use of an 'experimental technology' whereby the victim's memories, thoughts and consciousness(es) were uploaded into a computer mainframe.

Only one authority could be quoted as saying, 'the victims are all alive, but so far none have been able to make a statement, nor have they spoken since being freed." The same source was also quoted as saying, "The [perpetrator] that did this… who many know as Christopher Marshall, appears to have undergone the same procedure as his victims and still hasn't been available for comment."

Families of the victims have spoken to the media recently, stating that the news is "unbelievable" and they hope to have their friends and family home, safe again soon.

Episode 7

George and Brad are at Lucky's sipping Michelobs out of the bottle and watching the surfers catch the last few waves of the day. There's been a lull in new projects, compounding the already delicate situation with the writer's strike and various box-office flops. The only ones that can afford to go to the beach are the ones who've already given up, or who can afford to be picky.

Brad draws with his finger on the wooden bar, tracing the lines back into time, "You know this groove here could have been laid down six-hundred years ago."

"The ring you mean?"

"Yeah, the light ones are spring and summer, when there wasn't a lot of rain. The dark ones are winter and fall. We used to have warmer winters and wetter summers than we have now. The coast was a lot farther out too."

"When?"

"After the last ice age. I'mean, it's hard to say exactly."

"I was actually thinking of moving to Canada."

"Canada? Just for… the summer, or what?"

"All year, I'd like to see the snow. I'd like to see some elk, maybe drive a dogsled," says George.

"You thinking of retiring?"

"I'll admit. It's a little crazy right now. I could afford to get out. I'mean, I'm not obligated and I don't currently need the work."

"Is this about what happened at Marshalls?" says Brad.

"Not really, I've been thinking about it for a while. But it definitely doesn't improve matters."

"What do you know about it?" says Brad.

"Only what was in the papers."

"The papers? *The papers?* You read, *paper?*"

"I saw it on the second page and picked it up, why?"

Brad, incredulous, "*why* is because they aren't saying anything about what really happened."

"I gathered that from the article. Do you know something that they don't?" says George.

"Yeah… I'd says so. I was in Minton's office and overheard him talking to Cozens. It sounded pretty important, life or death, so I leaned in, but I could only make out a bit, so I followed Cozens to Republique, which was hard, considering I couldn't get parking, but anyway, I made it inside and found him at the bar. It looked like he wanted to get something off his chest, so after a couple three scotches he started to let it out. He said that in all likelihood we aren't going to be seeing any of them again."

"They got uploaded into a computer game like the SIMs right?" says George.

"Where did you hear that?"

"The Daily Breeze ran a story a few days ago, didn't you *read* it? They have an app you know."

"Anyway, yeah, they were hooked up to a server farm and downloaded onto a mainframe. Memories, personalities, everything."

"But how do they know, I mean, how does one communicate with a person in a computer?" says George.

"The same way as texting apparently, but I haven't tried those goggles yet, maybe that would work."

"What about facetime?"

Brad waggles his empty bottle, "the program he used didn't support regular streaming video, it was just a bunch of lines and static."

"But the voice comes through, right?"

"Yeah, but he said that Minton said it was a really creepy experience. You can't tell who is who."

"Sounds like hell," George, subdued.

"Huh, huh huh, *yeah*. He said they took the mainframe to Google to get it looked at, but who knows where it is now or who's got it. We'll probably never hear about it again."

"Who were they, did you get any names?" says George.

"Huh, huh-huh *ye-ahhhh*, that was the best part."

"Well?"

"You're not going to believe this. Luke Wilson, Monica Bellucci, Jimmy Fallon, and James Franco, plus like four more, but based on that..."

"Yeah, who knows."

"Who knows is right, it's gonna put a lot of studios in the red that are *already* in the red. I'mean they're not dead, but they might as well be."

"Just another reason to get ouotta here..."

"But wait, that's not all."

"No, I imagine not."

"The biggest mystery is that thing they saw before Jimmy disappeared."

"Thing?" says George.

"Yeah, a bunch of people said they saw a bigfoot. Even his brother, who he was with at the time, said it just came out of nowhere and grabbed him."

George doesn't have anything in his mouth but spits anyway, then quickly takes a drink and spits it out, "What? Bigfoot?"

"A lot of people said they saw it."

"And what about *you*?"

"What about me?"

"What do you think?"

"I don't know what I think, what do *yo-oou* think?"

"I *think*, they saw what everyone sees when they hang around here long enough. Eventually somebody in a costume is going to show up and kill someone, or kidnap them. Nothing surprises me anymore."

"So, you think it was just a guy in a costume?"

"Well, whatever it was it wasn't a bigfoot or... I can't even say it."

"What about the Patterson-Gimlin film?"

"You do a lot of research on this stuff?"

"But you've seen it, everyone's seen it."

"A-and it's been debunked."

"No, it hasn't. It's still officially unknown."

"The origin of the universe is still officially unknown," says George.

"Exactly."

"Yes, but that doesn't automatically mean that the other theory is true."

"Did you even *see* it! Its got delts, and quads. You can see the shoulder blades sliding around underneath the skin. Its even got breasts, so they can tell *it's a female*."

"If you are going to *per*sist in this subject, I'm going to *in*sist that I leave right now."

"But you're right. It's this place... Maybe *we're* the monsters."

"I don't buy that shit for a second. They didn't deserve what they got and there's no such thing, as monsters."

"I agree, I totally agree. I don't know what I think about monsters, but I don't dismiss it out of hand..."

George gives him a look like, are we really talking about this?

"...But whatever it was, it was *not* real. No definitely *not* real," says Brad.

"Do you know how many yahoos have access to old warehouses and movie sets. Somebody's uncle worked in the makeup department for *Vampires at Midnight*, or *An American Werewolf in London* and they get a three-hundred pound, six-foot five guy from Planet Fitness to go out on a Saturday night for a couple hundred bucks and an eight-ball of blow."

"That's right, that's the *only* explanation, and suits are even better now."

"I'm about done here, what about you?"

"Yeah, I should head home."

The breeze from the ocean is chilly beneath the silver sky. No one is on the beach save for a few surfers and videographers after some late afternoon b-roll.

Brad pulls the Piston's cap down over his eyes and strikes out across the parking lot. Ditto George in his grey suit and sunglasses, each knowing that it could have been them, but also secretly maintaining the belief that they are too high-powered, too well-connected to ever fall victim to something like that.

Brad turns up Serra onto Palm Canyon, waiting for the gate to close behind him before parking the Bentayga in the driveway. He gets out, pondering the mountains in the distance compared to his own finite time, when he notices some movement on the slopes. The sun has already set and this side of the hill is all in the shade, which is why he likes it here.

Something grunts behind him. He doesn't turn to look, slapping the soles of his sandals on the smooth pavement as he runs toward the hacienda. He's almost to the door when the thing grabs him, "Hey, heeeeeeyyyy! Put me down." His voice fading as he is bourne up and over the ridgeline. The dark, blurry shapes making a kind of cross as they disappear from view.

Stay tuned for more exciting episodes... of, *Famous Monsters*

104

Headed out, early morn after bear's breakfast of porridge, prepared by Goldilocks maid, not too much, just enough to make sure we're hungry for more, bear.

Crouched down, scanning hillsides, not to hide, to hunt, dressed in bear attire. Bear suit: to hunt bears.

Wool, wear bears loosely.

Father singing his favorite mondegreen misheard lyric, 'Born on the Bayou' to the tune of 'Travellin' Band' "runnin' down a hoodoo bear". Letting off indiscriminate rounds at the end of each "ye-ah!" line. Winchester .38 making an X with the bandolier across his chest embossed with the heraldic figure of a bear dressed as a man, paws held out, like a boxers'. Slogan reads: Garou Loup, Right to Arm Bears!

"What if we run out?" I say.

"Don't worry." He's Wolfen, hunting bear, unconcerned with trivial particulars. "We'll only need one. Here," he passes me the gun, kneeling beside me. "It's not a stick anymore son, it's a weapon. See how it's shaped like your hand from the outside, like it knows you're there, another 'phantom' limb alongside your own. You feel with it, look with it, aim with that notch there and that guide. Now take the other hand and move it into position underneath, pulling with exactly that force that will make it come to you."

Getting to the point slowly, the way fathers and patient teachers do, hours of instruction before you ever even get to see the gun let alone hold it. Then going through the procedure of loading and unloading it, taking it apart and putting it back together, carrying it around wherever you go and only then shooting it. It's a fact, he says, a lot of people who hold guns never even shoot them. Holding a gun is a whole 'nother matter than shooting it. Finger tensed at the brink of a decision. The aim and that gentle, deliberate pull. No movement wasted and no going back. It's only then, a few milliseconds before the gun goes off and you're brain's already sent the message to your finger—the time it takes to travel down your arm—that you think you want to change your mind, but by then that ship's already sailed, and, on the other end, that dog won't hunt... so you better know what you're doing.

I know this whole speech so well I could say it back to him with a few things added in since father taught it to son, like we don't need to kill bears anymore. Truth is, I never liked killing things or seeing them killed. I'd never even thought of it, yeah, really, but neither should you at my age. Not while I've still got it so good and no one's even had the chance to inconvenience me so much that I think of killing them, but to hunt an animal for sport is okay? aren't we animals too?

Father's got his hand over mine, anxious to hear that pop where it's supposed to come, at the end of a line, the completion of a thought.

"Ready. Fire on one, two... pow."

"What're we aiming at?" He says, after the ringing is gone.

"That stump."

"Which one?"

"That one," the one we'd hit.

"Nice job."

Talking shop while we walk, like for instance why a 12-gauge is called a 12-gauge, "You know the story... black sheep, black sheep have you any wool..."

"Yessir, yessir, three bags full."

"Well, a long time ago, the sheep would sell his wool, in bulk; three bags full. Wool is something sold by weight. As we say en francaise—avoir du pois, which means 'goods of weight', also the name of a system of measurement where a pound is 7000 Troy grains divided into 16 ounces. While twelve gauge is weighed in twelfths of a pound of lead. So that means there's a twelfth of a pound of lead in each one of these shells. It's not clear what the sheep meant by a 'bag' full, a 'bag' is not a unit of measure, but a woolsack is 26 stone, 14 pounds per stone is..."

"Three-hundred and sixty-four."

"That's right," patting me on the back. Paw praise.

This complicated way of assaying seems preposterous to us now, a remnant of a simpler if not less precise system, which always brings him back to his old bone with the British and their refusal to acknowledge their decline as a world power and mover. The empire 'upon which the sun never sets', consisting of a handful of protectorate states and their antiquated system of weights and measures, surviving if only to remind them of the grande olde days of spices, savages and exotic ports. Not to mention their appropriation of the logical, empirical measurement of the French and twisting it into something else[1]. And then their separatist sons with American aspirations went West and messed it up again and again in Canada and now it's really messed up. "But what really started it was when God gave them," he always refers to people as them, those people, and so forth, "permission to 'go forth and take all the birds of the air and fish of the sea' and basically take over the world by 'number and measure', which was Descartes' term, selling fruit out of the garden and walling it off so no one could get in and steal it. As soon as food stopped being free, so did we. They took us out of our home and into theirs, but they didn't take us all the way. There was still the big bad wolf who'd come, or so they say and steal a few of

---

[1]   It is widely known that the British are not very adept at French pronunciation, reflected by the small number of French loan words. Being perfectly conscious of this fact, the British have made a joke of their ignorance, intentionally pronouncing words wrong in order to head off the criticism of the French before they could raise it themselves.

their babies and raise them as his own. Not to eat, but to teach."

"What about the bulls and the boars?"

A slight hesitation, if I didn't know better, I'd say he was scared, "the bulls and the boars can never be tamed. We don't usually get that close to a bull, and if we do, we can run. Boars are different. They have authority. We don't go after them, they come after us."

We never kill a boar, they're like our Gods. They are fierce because it is their purpose to protect the animals of the forest. Where a bear is aggressive out of boredom and indifference, the boar's aggression comes from a place of wisdom, but also outrage that any should fail to appreciate the sanctity of the nature it is there to protect. The heart of a lion hidden in a swine's anatomy. Of course, they are rare here, even non-existent, but their mythology dates back to before we followed the tracks of the Sapes from Siberia to the New World. Sharing the hunt and occasionally taking credit for the kill.

Paw stops and sniffs, "smells like a Sape," our word for humans. Sapes, while they like to think of themselves as predators, in reality they are pretty pathetic when armed with a rock tied to a stick or any other weapon. A far shot, and a pretty bad one at that, from their Homo Habilis (Handy-man) ancestors. Those few remaining who still spend any time in the woods at all are the visionaries, romantics; societies' apostates, rhapsodizing the wolf's rogue wanderings as whimsical retreat, so unlike the automaton dunning of days that passes for life in the People, Person's, world.

They hunt too, but are generally the kind who hold guns rather than shoot them, their objective simply to be 'in the wild'. The gun serving only as an accessory, or protection when they go into more remote areas; mountains or ridgelines. Seeking high places for the same reasons as before, for security, so it's like they're coming back; where they think they want to be. Compensating for how unnatural the world has become. Which is why so many of them go missing. Thinking that just because they're out in the woods that they're closer to nature. You can literally see them a mile away, sitting on top of a pile of rocks just about as conspicuous as you can get, so it's like a whole town of them has descended, and the smell. That 'pine fresh scent', 'cool breeze', that doesn't smell anything like it's supposed to. It really puts you off your dinner, if you're lucky enough to find any… which makes paw angry for scaring them off, forgetting all the noise he had made earlier.

"I'm going to scare that Sape for spoiling our hunt."

He's not hard to find.

By the time they see us we're usually right on top of them and boy you should see them run. Other times we're like their best friend, appealing to our better nature of taking care of the weak, as we are sometimes known to do. Asking, will you teach us? We want to be-lieve, assuming a yoga-like posture before the one in whom he places so much faith, elevated above his own station to the height of guru, healer, or demigod.

Paw accedes all too readily to this type of adulation. Demonstrating that venerable snout, raised in appraisal or approval. "Yeahp, he's close, that bear. Right behin'd'ya'."

"Take me with you."

"Sure, if you can keep up?" Paw says, singing to himself as he bounds over shrubs and logs, "sneak-in' up on the – wind, b'fore its reach-ed the – end, back the way we – be-gin, do it all o'ver – a-gain."

I catch up with him a little ways on, settling into a new spot in the sun. Without turning he raises his paw and says, "beer."

"Here," handing him one from the bag.

"Chair, beer... now all we need is a bear."

"Got one Pa."

"Where?"

"No, a rhyme," part of the game we play while we're walking or waiting.

"Oaky then," pricking up his ears and leaning in like he's listening for the barest little sound over on the other side of the mountain.

"I sat on a map and had a little nap. Map, nap, sat."

"Not bad," sipping from his can as if it were a light airy brew, not a thick dark one, "mmhmm. Yes. I hadn't thought of it quite like that."

"O-or how about this? Huntin' bears, I sat down on a chair and had myself a beer. Chair, bear. There."

"A-ha!" hollars pa, "now that's a song," shifting in his chair as if he is about to get up, but stays seated, "where's that Sape. Did you scare him?"

"He didn't have a gun."

"He shouldn't be out here without a gun, should 'e son? What do we say when we see a Sape in the woods?"

"W-w-which w-way d-d-did he go?"

"What about a deer?"

"We say hi to a deer because she's our aunt."

Questions and answers, then numbers up to a thousand, repeating the sequence all day. My job is to get the bear's attention. Hunting's supposed to be a wolf's most sacred institution, but hunting isn't really hunting if all you're there for is bait.

"Wouldn't it be easier to use honey, one tablespoon will attract friend Bruin more than a half a dozen…"

"Too late for that, he can smell you already. Now go put on that suit and come back out here when you're ready," packing up his chair and empties.

Sape suit: clean white sweater and pants, some old socks and a hat, 'Bruins'.

I can sense him out there, moving with a self-assurance that displaces all obstacles. His apparent clumsiness really an exquisite kind of grace (for a bear). Handles himself the way he handles everything else, with a lazy kind of circumspection, casually bumping into things as if to test their substantiality. How easily they break, how hard they fall.

Paw unscrews the top of his flask and takes a whiff, "now put some o' this on." Eau de Sapiens cologne. "Wait'll he gets a whiff o' this," which will be anytime now. I can't act natural knowing that something is going to happen. But paw says this is the surest way to catch a bear. That is, if he comes. Finally it's too much, "I'm outta here," ripping off the shirt and hat and running off in the direction of nearest town.

Father catches up with me on the road, if anything because I let him. The problem with him still being so young (only eleven years out of stock) is that he's partly in the glory of his first 'hunt' as we say, and partly in that of his son, as if the hunts of his son were hunts of his own. Taking credit for the things I do, if I'm right, or claiming that I did it wrong, if I'm not. Qualifying every move I make until I'm strong enough to beat him, which I can't, demonstrating this fact by picking me up. Nothing I'm hating more.

"Put me down," my voice cracking with strain and anger as I reach over his shoulder and pull his shirt over his head. His uncoordinated weight bringing us both to the ground just in time to be embarrassed by a busload of Sape kids on their way to school. The bus slowing to a stop once the driver sees that I mean to get on, leaving Paw in an attitude of thwarted vigor, deflated but not defeated. Lamenting the younger generation's indifference toward the institutions of the old; less Loup than Garou.

The day's hunt nearly foiled, but determined to finish it, Paw lopes back up the hill, tracks down the bear that we had been stalking and does it in with several quick slashes of his claws before the bear can land any of its own. Trying for a selfie, he takes a few pictures with the bear, standing too close and leaning too far into the frame so all he gets is some indistinguishable fur and the left side of his face.

Unlike Sapes, Wolfen don't make up stories about their conquests and exploits, exaggerating some while diminishing others—at least not about something as sacred as the hunt, choosing instead to preserve virtue and humility over personal prestige. Insulting the meat, claiming that it was smaller than it actually was so the story of the smallest, scrawniest bear is often the best.

It offends us when Sapes resort to less intrepid modes of combat, like shooting a fleeing animal in order to 'save the hunt'. Sometimes the hunt is left, which is called 'leaving the hunt' when the animal is lame or tries to flee, as shooting one's prey in flight is considered cowardly. Of course, there are weeks when one doesn't need meat, but Wolfen are expected to go out anyway and either teach their stock to hunt or get a picture of themselves with a bear[2].

The modifier stock is a suffix. The -stock drops around the same time the voice does. As children, both stocks and Sapes are told that monsters do exist so it isn't as much of a shock when they encounter one. The hardest part isn't accepting the reality of such things as much as it is recognizing them when we see them, since many monsters don't look all that different than us. There have always been different species and differences within species sufficient to become species of their own. The greater the difference, the greater the reaction to that difference, be it shock, fear, anger or something else, like attraction. It's not often that different species or groups within species encounter each other without incident, whether in an urban setting or in the wild. Most of the time it comes down to disputes over territory. Similar species will compete for food and living arrangements, while dissimilar ones will have developed such specialized habits that they may not even think of competing. It all comes down to the difference.

---

[2]   rules state that the camera must not exceed 8 megapixels or carry a telephoto lens.

Wolfenstock

All animals possess at least some sense of themselves, even insects. They may not be aware of the concept of death, but they do fear it, that feeling again when the whole herd scatters. Their ability to live in a dangerous and sometimes inhospitable environment depends on their resistance to and avoidance of those factors not in keeping with the principles that sustain life, dying only in the process of trying to defy it. 'Because I could not stop for death – He kindly stopped for me[3]'. This being another one of Paw's sayings; 'a saying for everything and always has something to say', like 'for everything that dies something else is fed', 'what's good for one is bad for the other', 'never kill more than you can eat', 'there's always somebody faster' to which we might add, 'running is just an invitation to chase'.

If it wasn't for the Wolfen's insistence on tradition at the expense of more worldly concerns, perhaps Sapiens wouldn't have survived as long as they have, seeing which of the weak the toughest, which of the dumb the brightest. Saving them from the belief that they were the most intelligent thing in the universe; the only animal that could think, feel and speak.

On the surface it seems like a fully integrated society, with very little violence cross species, but fear of the stranger still exists, however unconscious, in Sapien psychology. Their reaction to the sight of the long dark hair, the lean, mean physique of a hunter and devoted runner that still occasionally eats with its hands, tears meat and licks its fur in public.

---

[3] Dickinson, Emily. "Because I could not stop for Death." The Academy of American Poets. Web. http://www.poets.org/poetsorg/poem/because-i-could-not-stop-death-712/

Because of their size, Wolfen generally occupy the more physically demanding jobs, but up until maturity, stocks and Sapes work, play and learn alongside each other. Differences between species are acknowledged, but not emphasized and all are encouraged to study similar things. Lessons are typically delivered visually through pre-recorded 'movies'. Anything not actually happening in real time is called a movie. In fact, school consists almost entirely of movies. Stilted low-budget productions designed to instruct not to entertain. Every gesture and word reduced to its most derivative element. The audience intently disinterested, watching for the entertainment factor in material that is anything but. Titles like 'Safe Hunting Is No Accident', instructing stock in the dangers of going out to hunt (stalk) alone; 'The bull, the boar and the bear' religious theology and 'Roadkill: Don't play in the road' describing the grisly effects of excess traffic on our rural roads. I fall asleep half way through 'Roadkill: Don't play in the road', my dream of beer and bears interrupted by the bell; time for a sweet snack before English, which I like because I read a lot. Only a small part of our education actually comes from books, which are usually read by oneself—considering that books take a long time to read—but that's okay because at least reading gives me some time alone. Usually an hour or two before dinner and again before bed. Dinner usually consisting of BBQ, or 'fast food'—an impromptu hunt. People following their noses to wherever the food has started cooking first.

After dinner the parents go out and the kids stay home to look after themselves. Their idea of babysitting; that the more kids there are, the more they'll be seen (at least by each other) and like they say, 'children should be seen and not heard'. The oldest or more aggressive kids locking the younger ones in closets or rooms so they can watch late night movies or play games with more adult themes. Little bros and sisters, not looking a whole lot different than Sape friends, dressed up as 'wild things', with painted faces and heraldic hides. Keeping themselves busy while I go pick my parents up from the bar. I've been driving for over three years, but only ever got my real license in March. Stocks qualify a year earlier than Sapes. Stocks having better depth perception and risk assessment, which also means they're more precocious when it comes to taking care of themselves. Last time I babysat I found them burning furniture in the stove, saying that they were 'feeding grampa'. Ancestors can be pretty demanding when it comes to tradition and these days it seems to take less and less to piss them off.

The bar is full of smoke and at least twenty different varieties of perfume from sour-piquant to 'bottled mummy'; vaguely sweet with notes of formaldehyde. I'm allowed to come in as long as I promise not to drink. Every time I come here—which is nearly every night—I have to tell the bouncer 'Rusty' (who still pretends not to know who I am) that I'm here to pick up my parents and that even I've got better things to do that sit around in a smoke-filled room drinking overpriced beer. I'mean, where do adults get the idea that every time a kid comes near a drink that they automatically want to snuffle it. What kind of thrill could I possibly get? Us kids already do almost everything they do. Why would I want to listen to old people listen to new music or old people listen to old music? Especially when it costs five dollars for a pint or a bottle, one of those avoirdupois, that sells for no more than two-dollars and fifty cents at a store? Even with only three or four of those a day, that's 2.50 × 4 is 10 bucks times 7 is... seventy bucks a week. That's my tuition guys, so while I have to work some odd job to make some extra money, they get to sit there respectable and content in their culturally sanctioned condition of drunkenness, but even if I don't get into a good university, at least I can go to college, which will prove—if only to me—that I am my own person, separate and distinct from those old, moldy traditions and making the old man happy. Be he the old man, or old wolf, who died thousands of years ago in some long, forgotten war of the bulls and the boars. The incoherent story of our people, incoherent because whenever someone starts telling it, they slur their words, mumbling and grumbling their way through even if they're completely sober, so nobody knows how it ends or even what happens half the time, it's just the way the story's told.

The bartender, acknowledging that I'm still here and looking surprised about it, waves me through to a booth in the back where my parents are sitting with three other Sapes, talking about fixing the boat, moving to the woods, getting in the RV and driving to South America.

"Do you want a ride home?" I say.

No, they say, we've got our own ride... place doesn't close 'til 1:00... people we just met... forget their names... we want to stay.

"Can we stay? Can we?"

Sure, why don't you stay forever.

The house is quiet when I get back: no TeeVee or video games means trouble.

"Kids? Guys? Where are you?"

I find them in the big room downstairs, the one we use for bouncing and drying out, huddled in a circle round the dog, which has pulled itself part way into the closet in an effort to escape its tormentors, Canis Stock-Major lying prostrate in an attitude of prayer, or praying, oh dog, let my soul be free.

"Leave that thing alone," I say. "It doesn't like it."

They don't respond. Don't even look up, just go on torturing the poor animal that already looks dead.

Poor dogsbody. She kicked the bucket.

Oh, great.

They're sitting very close so I have to lean in to see what they're doing. Hard to see or even believe, but what they are doing is, is they're licking the saliva and whatever, goo, from the corners of the dog's mouth. Its flesh dissolved (or eaten away?) in pink goo by-product of the process. Muscles pulled taut over a frame like a tennis racket that I see now actually is a tennis racket; catgut inextricably caught up with its own gut. Teeth's firm grip on the handle, eyes bugged out in avid chew and confusion.

I scream at them, "kids get out of there." Looking up at me with terrible eyes all gone black, black goo.

High strangeness, like holes opened up for strange things to come through. Not even asking to be invited, just come on in without knocking or availing themselves of the door even, just right through the wall and sometimes without even seeming to notice.

Disgusted, I pick them up by little arms and legs and fling them out of the room. Kids go bouncing off the walls, the ceiling, the floor. No crying or complaints, probably don't even feel it, just part of the fun before segueing into the next thing, which is 'feeding grampa'. I don't realize it until I hear the furnace open and shut.

They're bringing firewood in by the armful and loading it into the furnace.

"No, it's too hot. It's going to explode." The heat blasting out with a kind of sound; a hot aspirate breath that devours itself almost immediately.

"Don't sit so close," I say. "You'll go blind." But it's useless. They can't hear me. Transfixed by the glow of the flames. Faces of dead relatives floating up in convection currents like images on the TeeVee. The only way to get their attention is to shut it off, but it's not that simple. There are actually two furnaces so if one goes out, or gets too hot, the other can take over. Shutting it down is dangerous. Usually you'd need two people to do it, turning the heat down in one while regulating the heat in the other, but something has taken control, meaning to do some damage it seems.

I run back and forth, opening the flue on one furnace, while trying, unsuccessfully, to open it at the same time on the other, until I nearly go out of body from the exertion. Sweat has covered my face, though it only takes a minute or two of running up and down the hall until the balance is restored. The faces in the glass fading and then subsiding just before the flame dies out. The kids take off again, postponing their mischief here to start it anew somewhere else.

"Kids?" I say, pausing to listen, "where are you?"

Footsteps upstairs, voices muffled in hushed co-operation. A pot crashes to the floor, the sound of a table being dragged. How much trouble can you get into in the kitchen? A lot it seems... Admitting, finally that I can't do this on my own, but the only person I can call is Cammy; 'Commando Cammy' because she likes to hunt and drives a Camaro. She agrees to come over, even though it's past her Sape bedtime.

I wait for her outside, the thrum of the Camaro's engine audible long before she comes into view.

"What's going on?" she says.

"We've got a situation."

"What kind of situation?"

"I can't really explain, you'd have to see for yourself."

We enter the house, noting the crepuscular gloom, the ambient banging, following the sound to the kitchen where the kids are precariously balancing chairs and appliances on the table and on the appliances and juggling knives.

"Where's the dog?" she says.

I point to the door and the stairs leading to the basement. She gives me a worried look and starts down, letting out a little shriek of horror, "gross."

"Here lies poor dog's body."

"We'll miss him," says Cammy.

"We'll miss him," says a chorus of children. They seem much more docile now, the first signs of transubstantiation beginning to appear on the face and hands of the Sape kids.

"Okay, let's go."

"Where?" says Cammy.

"The woods. We can't be here when their parents get back."

"Where're we going?" says little brother.

"To hunt bears."

Getting them ready is easier than I thought, they actually want to go, using sticks for guns and bags for beer. There isn't enough room in the car for everybody so we have to tie a few to the roof. Squealing in delight as Cammy maneuvers round corners, driving as fast as she can before anyone notices, which is pretty hard to do.

The woods aren't far, but we have to pass the tire store and a gas station first. Luckily no one is out tonight. Surface streets deserted, except for a tow truck that slows beside us, but keeps going.

Cammy turns onto a dirt road, avoiding potholes and bumps as we climb to the top of a hill. This is as far as we can go. From here we see the town below, always larger than I think it is. Although lots of people come here, hardly anyone takes the east trail, mostly because it's so flat for so long. Starting out in a heavily wooded area and thinning towards the treeline as we gradually rise in altitude, not pronounced, but just enough to lull you into a kind of meditative stupor before you realize that your legs are getting tired and you didn't bring nearly enough water, or you change your mind at the last second and decide to turn around.

I've been this way before, but never all the way, though it looks like I'll have to now because it goes without saying, I can't very well go back. Taking responsibility for these kids who are now setting off flares, fireworks and homemade grenades. Laying a candy-coloured trail and scaring away all the bears, but what can you expect, things don't stay the same and kids don't grow up overnight.

The trail forks into several paths: over the mountain; around the mountain; and back to town. Even though I'm the only one going, we take the path over. The way marked with abandoned Sape camps; some with bodies still in them, leaning against trees or sitting upright in chairs, surrounded by empty beer cans. Signs say 'Welcome to Camp Can't Hack It', 'Keep Practicing or Go Home' and 'The Land of The Dead'. The trail becoming indistinguishable from the surrounding forest as we head farther East; where all trails eventually end.

The stock are the first to leave. Heading off in alternate directions, chasing the scent of bears. The Sape kids stay until their transformation is complete. They are only a few hours behind. The last one fully transforming just before sunrise.

Cammy stays with me as long as she can. We come out in a clearing just before the final rise to the summit. I tell her I'll get in touch with her on the other side. It's almost noon, which means it'll be dark again by the time I reach the top. The rapid declension of light reducing my problems to the most essential: food and a place to sleep.

I watch Cammy until she disappears back into the treeline. Staring after her to the valley and the green gray blur of the sea in one direction and the bald peaks of the mountain in the other.

The hunters will be out by now, following the trail I have left for them.

I hold my head up, sniff the air and listen.

124

The Longest Day

It's more likely you'll see a zombie, stoned or on the road. Like the time I died. Early one morning, end of December. The feeling of the weather the moment you die is always the same. If I could recommend the best time, I'd say mid-July.

A friend and I are sitting, smoking a joint on the hood of a neighbor's car. A carload of teenagers drive by, "hey punks."

We throw snowballs at them, "pug off".

The neighbor sees us and hollers, "get off my car."

We jeer at him as we ride away. Skirting the black ice on the shoulder of the road.

We wouldn't have turned to crime if everything around us wasn't already a crime. Countries built on injustice and covered up by violence to keep anyone from finding out.

A crime only being a 'crime' to prevent someone else from doing it. As we all know, there are two sets of rules; one for us and one for them.

That's what crime has, that lawful activity doesn't. It makes the first move while the recipient is always reacting to what has already been done and doesn't know what to expect next.

They come out of the woodwork at odd hours. Just when you think you're alone... turn into real disagreeable characters. Pound down doors, crawl through barred windows, call on the phone, borrow loans, won't take no answer for an answer... Magicians who turn everything they touch into stone. Burning down the house while they're still inside.

Leaflets torn from the book of revelations; scenes from Brughel's 'Hell-on-Earth' flutter down like ashes from the campfires of hell. Or is that just snow? It's hard to tell anymore.

It all moves so slowly. Even them, forever poised like they're going to attack. Skin stretched, barely adhering to bone. Their entire lifeforce concentrated in this one act, becoming nearly weightless. Betrayed by the stilled pulse and absence of breath as they drift past. Striking with a single, efficient squeak as the jaw opens up and the teeth sink in. Adrenalin spiking in the victim's veins; a mix of codeine itch and cold water shock. The heart slows, like time, until it stops. The way all things do. Notice how they never move on their own. Bodies that have long since stopped working, but go on anyway. While the living struggle to keep up.

Crows in mourning plumage croon over black hole graves. Little hell babies hacking through the frozen ground with hatchets and hammers. Frogs leaping from their throats, gripped in rigor mortis grins.

A dog barks, a baby cries, a boy yells back intermittently, an indeterminable distance away.

Lady laments—lays awake.

A man pulls out a knife, switchblade catching flames in its web of slaying, waiting like slow bleeding inside the skull.

People hopscotch down narrow alleyways holding hands. Skipping cracks, circumnavigating ever-encroaching pools of blood from Johnson's breached artery. Skirting past junkies hunkered down and out in doorway bunkers, contagious in close proximity to blood-spattered walls, hematoma, urine flowing from liquid viscera, seams in the street under which ancient rivers still, on occasion, flow, dividing the city into a star pentacle pie.

Zombies hanging out in all night diners wearing the same service station shirt from where he works under dusty trench coat jacket smeared with gouts of ketchup and mustard, like you're more likely to see a zombie stoned or on the road. Sometimes they don't even slow down to shoot.

We're down at the waterfront, some friends and I, watching waves crash against the shore and wall.

Some kind of announcement crackles through the loudspeakers I hadn't even realized were there, as the street lights come on in a different shade of white, almost blue.

"This is the science lab. I just saw the biggest boat I've ever seen capsized by a giant wave. Evacuate all beach side residences and locations, I repeat…"

A sucking sound reaches our ears as the tide rolls out and comes back with a roar, washing logs onto the road. Water splashes our heels as we climb the stairs to the car. The waves are getting bigger now, a wall of water forming about a kilometer out. The sun partially obscured, shining through a translucent dish held up to the sky, bobbing over the rim and shining squarely down, glinting off wet streets; the sea.

We reach the top of a hill and watch the waves roll in and out, forming a kind of moat around us before settling back into their customary position.

Just before last call making trips back and forth between the bars, cause for alarm there is something going on in the harbour. The sound came first like exploding pipe bombs on Canada Day, or the distant thunder of an incoming tropical storm, flashing white lights through the trees. Bright and growing brighter until it was as bright as day and just as suddenly going out, leaving us in a dark, darker than before with all the colour washed out.

Then the snow came, or was it ash? The longest day; the day I died.

All the hands on the clocks stopping at once, until even the numbers themselves became meaningless. Sinking into the face to reemerge as sixes, spinning on their axes as if the universe had reconsidered its stance on time, no longer a function of the cosmos.

We walk back to the waterfront. Ships disguised as islands float off shore. Bolts of lighting cross between them, shooting up fireworks from the center and radiating out, accompanied by low booming sounds, giving the illusion of distance.

Storm clouds obscure circling ships. Intercontinental offspring of mother hurricane, harbour near clusters of ships and docking lights.

The islands progressively draw nearer, ushered by rain laden cirrus.

Clouds fill our head, sealing sutures, blocking foramina. Alpha males turn to cowards losing fortitude defending fertile womb, no longer able to stand up to the threat.

Some spineless idiot speaks, "you can have this place that nobody wants, if you want."

"We will take it and every other island spit, shit hill on this planet," comes the response.

All of a sudden there's some great interest in planet Earth, as if we didn't know it was there until we could barely see it, hidden behind the light of the world that seemed to blot out the sun.

"No!" they cry, "you can't have it." Looking up from their various circumstances to see what they had been missing; that in order to lift themselves up, they have to lift others up as well. So close to the Earth, it's hard to feel its attraction. Pleading with each other, *we can change. We'll never take you for granted again. Nothing is more important. Please forgive us.*

The colour slowly starts to return, grass grows, the days get shorter and longer. We feel hot and cold. Fear and joy. Yearning and fulfillment. A perfect if not ideal balance of opposites, which keeps the world and everything in it from collapsing. Each of us understanding this for ourselves, vowing, never to look at it in any other way, again.

The Heavy Metal Sound of Steel

Cheap speakers carve out hollow sounds battering metal panels. Engine noise tears through injectors, tight titanium tubes. Harold shakes his fist to the music. The fuel gauge sinks as he stomps the pedal, passing a tractor on a double solid line.

Cars doppler past giving sharp, exaggerated jabs of their horns. Headlights sweeping a continuous wash of concrete coming to an end in ten, nine, eight... The implacable whoosh of wheels cuts out as the ground falls away, nothing but the tops of trees, houses and the blue-black of the bay. From below it would look like a small plane taking off (a short flight) before dropping into the steep grade, forcing an involuntary *whoop*. The wheel bites into his hand like a captured animal seeking to free itself from the yoke of the road. He leans back, elbows bent, holding steady at 10 and 2. Not a bit nervous, he's done this before.

Borrowed lights of reflectors rear up at the bottom of the hill. He pulls into the driveway of a middle-class suburban home on the beach, but with no waterfront or sand in the yard. After a shower he brushes and shaves, mirror mouthing the words to a ballad like a kissing incantation, recreating the events of Saturday night/ Sunday last. The way she gazed up at him before they kissed on the dance floor. The pupils that sucked up everything in the room, including her, so she had to feel around in the dark. Exhilarated by the prospect of her first time and a calculated fear of intimacy. Arcane pleasures that until then had been forbidden and she wasn't sure how she would react. He squeezes his eyes shut to keep the vision from dissolving, but she recedes into the dark corner of the roadhouse.

In a hurry he eats whatever's available and heads back out to the car. Sliding across the leather, gripping the gearshift, fingering the emblem on the handle. Porthole vents, four on either side of the engine compartment, light up in festive firing order of red, orange, green, blue blowing leaves off the paved drive as he backs onto the street. Idling up to the light and accelerating on yellow only a fraction of a second before it turns red, keeping up his speed for as long as he can without letting it go below thirty.

A police cruiser signals him to yield with a single squelch of its siren. Harold slows to the shoulder. The cruiser speeds past before he's had time to come to a complete stop. Only slightly inconvenienced, he regains his momentum and pulls onto a side street.

Lights flash through sight lines ahead and to the right. A crowd is gathered behind a cordon of yellow tape enclosing two crashed cars. Ambulance attendants roll stretchers into waiting ambulances slow and methodical; there are no lives to save. Harold circles the scene twice looking for a place to park. The ambulances leave sans sirens, freeing the entrance to the main plaza parking lot.

Harold gazes at his reflection in the rearview, considering what he should say, how he should walk in, how much money he is prepared to spend. But unlike the perfectly jelled part in his hair, words and actions are not things he can perfect in the mirror.

He climbs out, checking several times to see if the door is locked.

Columns of light pour down waxed metal bodies; dark, blotchy outlines spaced evenly apart. Tow trucks haul the wrecked cars away. Harold pulls up his collar, digs his fists into his leather jacket and strolls into the street. A General Motors insignia lies athwart the centerline. Harold bends down and tucks the artifact into his pocket.

Headlights flash around the corner.

He strides on.

Another set of headlights emerge from the opposite direction, engulfing him in their intimidating light. He makes a dash for the sidewalk as the two cars collide in sounds of screeching metal.

He feels pain and is jolted into a dark space, oriented by a single beam of light, contrapuntal to the surrounding darkness; a glowing apparition reaching out in a white wave. Sharp, prickly fingers prod impossibly close to the skin with the numbness of blood starting to recirculate after having stopped for the first time ever. No memory of leaving or being away, just a sudden return that makes the place he's returning to seem less real.

Lights shine on his body sprawled out in the grass. A new crowd has assembled consisting of members from the first with the addition of a few new disaster junkies. Standing motionless in the impartial stupor of an uneventful evening. He feels himself rise and stroll effortlessly across the street.

Sendozen's begins to clear out around 23:00, about the time the last band goes on and impatient teens take leave. Harold crouches low in the driver's seat, watching lovers beeline for cars, noting each peacoat and frocked figure until he spots Louise talking to Travis by the door. She passes him something and leaves with her girlfriends. Travis lingers thoughtfully for a moment, studying the object in his hand and strolls off in the opposite direction. Taking his time with a sweep and a hop in his step. Harold watches until he is out of view then follows him down a quiet residential street. Lights in the porthole vents flicker with the touch of a nervous foot. Travis spins round, enveloped in the cold, impersonal glare of headlights. The impact throws him to the ground. He screams, clutching at his knee. Harold drives over him, one, two more times before speeding out of town. The route laid out in his mind, taking him from the brightly lit agora into the rural wilds where his acts would resemble more the ambivalent works of nature.

A stop sign rears up at an intersection. Harold spots a pedestrian crossing the road. The pedestrian hobbles on, assured of the basic goodness of his fellow man to stop at the designated place. Harold hits the breaks, coming to a stop only a few feet from the man. Their eyes meet. Terror creases the man's face. He shrieks, cursing drunken slurs, bringing his cane down repeatedly on the hood of the car. Harold experiences a sense of apathy and contempt towards the man resulting from his repulsive disposition and way of conducting himself more than his idiotic words. He hesitates for a moment before stomping the pedal, sending the old man tumbling into a ditch at the edge of a farmer's field. Headlights shine on the crumpled body. Dark blood oozes from his mouth and nose, he moans.

Satisfied, Harold turns on the radio. The radio responds with the roar of blacklisted American Rock 'n' Roll on a pirate station.

Headlights approach from behind. He kills the lights, pulls a U-turn and heads back into town, a phantom wind roaring past the oncoming vehicle.

Inside, a man in a cowboy hat has his radio tuned to a country station. He hears the car pass, feels its velocity but doesn't see. Cursing, the cowboy stomps the brakes, turns off the radio, rolls down the window, leans out and listens. Engine sounds fade into the night. He pivots on his seat throwing one cowboy-footed boot onto the road. Crickets chirp in an adjacent field. Wind rattles corn stalks, their blades anointed with the thinly broadcasted light of the moon. He heaves a contemplative breath as if the air still held a description of the car and its driver. His job demands a relentless attention to detail. He waits for it. The air is fresh but not instructive.

Road hog clouds tumble in from the east. He'd give them a ticket if he could. A single droplet strikes his cheek. He slams the door, turns up the music and drives on.

Dry thrills and screams along the roadside.

A deer jumps in front of the headlights, sending a shockwave through the steel compartment. Harold fishtails onto the soft shoulder and races faster, asserting his control. Out of bounds of the mind with no limits under the hood. Taking eyes off the road and feeling direction's attraction.

"Get out of my way," he yells at nothing.

Aiming through the gun-sight hood ornament he hits a man stepping off a sidewalk and sideswipes a moving car into the guardrails. Sparks fly out in an array. The driver stares at him in mid-scream. Harold grinds the vehicles together with sharp jabs of the wheel and releases seconds before the rail ends. The driver takes immediate corrective action, overcompensating for the sudden change in trajectory, wheels biting into the soft grass, dragging the car down, flipping once before slamming into a tree.

Harold glances back to see glass and bits of metal fly.

It's light out when he comes to. Head between the seat and the driver's side window. He doesn't remember much, if anything, from the night before. He had gone to meet Louise at the bar. He left his car in the parking lot and was about to cross the street. That's about it. From what he sees of his surroundings, he guesses he must be somewhere north of town, along a lonely stretch of road with farms on either side. There doesn't seem to be anyone out, which is great news for him. The car is in pretty bad shape. One side is significantly bashed in. There are blood stains on the hood and different colours of paint on the doors and quarter panels. He wipes the blood off with a rag and drives to the body shop where he works, suspiciously obeying all traffic laws.

The repairs will take a couple of days so he catches a bus home, trying to recall the details of the previous night, but all he can think about is the car, part graduation present part loan and what his parents will say when he returns without it. Getting them to lend him the money took a lot of convincing and then he had to sit through their long droning admonitions. *Cars are dangerous. Cars are not toys. No screeching of tires. No speeding. Wear a seatbelt.*

Acting natural, Harold strolls into the house and aims for the fridge. Breezing past his father reading the paper open to an inner section.

"Mornin' son. Just getting in? You must have had quite a night," lowering the page to peer over the fringe.

The television is audible in the next room amid the quiet rustling of his mother at her painting.

Harold responds through a mouthful of potato salad, "working late at the shop… mmm went out with Louise… stayed over at her place."

"Do anything special or just go out?"

Harold pours himself a glass of milk. "We saw 'Space Explorers... mmm mmm. Two'."

"Really? I haven't heard of it," Harold's father studies his son's face and returns to his newspaper with scrutiny. Sounds of congenial conversation summon mother to the kitchen, hub of family life dressed in night attire. She looks at them then out onto the street, "Where's the car?"

"The fuel pump blew so I had to get it towed, I'll pick it up later tonight."

"Oh my gosh, what happened? Is everything alright?"

"Of course, I just lost power, the engine wasn't getting any uh, gas," Harold concerns himself with his milk. Watching it coat the inside of the glass. His face lights up Tilt.

"You sure it's just the fuel pump?" asks his father.

"Yeah, gas was spurting out. I had to tie it down with, uh... panty hose and idle all the way back to the shop. It's on the lift right now."

Harold takes his glass and strolls into the living room, pretending to look at pictures hanging in their neat wooden frames.

News of the hit-and-runs spreads rapidly around town. Four dead and five injured. The press is describing it as a serial road rampage blood-fest, a lead that keeps on bleeding. Words fly into print without proper substantiation, soon everyone has an alternate version of the truth.

"I don't even know if we can call these incidents hit and runs. There is neither word nor definition to describe this breed of driving. I'mean how could anyone be so blatantly and brutally sadistic? It makes me wonder if this isn't the beginning of a new age of criminals, breaking every mortal law of man and Jesus."

"What're you gonna do Len?" asks a tin cop voice.

"Take him down," Len, fist-pounding the bullpen desk the two men share, "Can't let vermin like that walk the streets."

"I don't think the captain's gonna assign you to the case. You're working the bank robbery and that case is supposed to be closed in the next thirty-six…"

"Never mind. I'm gonna catch this freak and you're gonna do the paper work on the robberies otherwise I'm gonna kick your rookie wise ass, you got it?"

"Yessir," replies the obsequious cop.

Len gets up in a huff, stomping over to take in a serene view of the Lake and environs.

"How can I know what's going on when all I see are ducks on the water. I'm looking in the wrong direction entirely. I may as well be staring at the wall, get a lot more done."

He reels away from the idyllic scene, turning several heads on his way out of the building.

Onset evening is attended by a gentle pattering of rain. Harold catches a bus downtown and steals a 56' El Camino, cruising Dallas to Ross Bay circling the cemetery twice before looping back through Fernwood and into the stomping grounds, West Saanich, highway 17A.

He kills the lights and turns onto Beaver Lake road, scanning the airwaves for some appropriate music, but finds only the usual pop, country, jazz—gumdrops and lollipops. Whatever he's looking for, it isn't there yet, lying dormant between the stations. Sounds that he imagines might resemble some sort of polygon, not the smooth corners of contemporary life, but a geometry all its own. A topography of creases and dents, like an aluminum can whose pressure has suddenly and unevenly been released, producing the sounds of crumpled metal.

The parking lot is not quite deserted; a few cars with heads pressed together, windows fogged up, others appear empty. He parks in the open and strolls down to the shore.

A man stops him on the path, "have you seen a little dog?"

Harold shrugs.

The man toddles off calling a dog's name.

The water audible before it comes into view, slapping the shore and retaining wall of the lower path. Harold stares long and deep, a projection or exchange of something mental over the lake. At length he removes his clothes and swims out until he is somewhere near the center. The shore located only by the croak of crickets and toads that seem to have hopped up a trellis of fog and are now suspended above him. He stays only as long as necessary, until the exchange is complete.

His is the only vehicle left in the lot. He switches on the high beams that do nothing for navigation and eases back onto the highway. Cruising to the bay on the other side of the peninsula and back.

The air begins to clear as he nears town again, passing the lake on the right and merging onto the highway. Taillights glow about a kilometer away. He rushes to catch up, falling in behind his quarry, a Buick of equal size and weight. The occupant either doesn't see him or doesn't care as Harold pulls up next to them on a double solid line. The driver slows a bit, making way for Harold to pass. They go on like this for about a quarter of a mile, the driver of the other car intermittently glancing over, waving him on. Harold smiles and waves back, giving the car a nudge on the rear fender. The driver raises an outraged hand and slams it down, mouth working behind deaf glass, keeping one eye on the road. Harold swerves again, hitting the car in the same spot. Abandoning all hope of reasoning with his tormentor the besieged driver accelerates, leaning into the wheel. Harold is only too happy to follow. Hitting it harder this time on the rear passenger side door. The car shoves back, grinding metal against metal.

Harold whoops. Listening for the nuances in the sound, the interior a resonant cavity for deeper bass tones, building until it abruptly cuts out. He glances over to see the other party swerve onto a side street. Harold in his transport misses the turn and skids to a stop in the middle of the road. Losing time and speed, he pulls a U-ey and jumps the curb, catching up with his quarry at the next light, squeezing through a window of green, while Harold, confident in his abilities goes on yellow then red. The intersection clear both ways.

His quarry races faster, but is sloppy at handling, going wide round the corners and making too frequent use of his breaks. Harold, the bolder of the two, turns into the parallel lane. Taking the S-curve straight so he doesn't have to slow down. The lake comes into view on the right, giving the impression of open space. Harold waits until they are wheel to wheel and slams into the other car, perhaps a little harder than he expected, sending them both careering down the bank. The impact slows him a little, landing in some brambles along the shore. He rolls down the window and climbs onto the roof in time to see the other car go under with a gurgling *blurp* and rising bubble of air. Harold holds his breath, waiting to see if the driver, whoever he is, surfaces in time. Either he went down with the car or swam a ways and came up in the reeds. It doesn't matter. What he needs now is a ride. He scrambles up the bank and scans the street for a car to steal.

Perplexed but undeterred, Len visits and revisits crime scenes with gloves and kit. Taking paint samples from scored quarter panels, seeking and interviewing witnesses, spotting men he sees as suspicious and following them out of buildings, down streets into cars. Examining every vehicle on the road for the identical shade of black paint or any other telltale sign, a scratch or a dent, a maniac at the wheel. No one seems to remember anything.

Len infers that the murderer must be from out of town. He spends hours on the phone to other cities, towns, provinces, countries; a long strenuous paper trail ensues.

Almost every broadcast leads with stories on the killings, the most recent one taking place just a few hundred feet from the station itself. Reporters have set up a kind of camp around the perimeter of the lake.

but nobody is saying anything. Except of course when Len yelled a reporter right into his car and ripped the cameraman's film out, saying, "get your all-seeing eye outta my face," Len's not so covert way of eschewing all suspicion by accusing the other of muckraking. But they knew, they all did, that something was about to happen—had been happening—for a while now, but had simply gone unnoticed. Hidden under the auspices of coincidence, accident, the inability for anyone to make the connection and see it for what it was.

On the fifth day the police receive an anonymous letter. Hastily written characters scrawled across the page spelling out the intimate thoughts of a madman:

My uncanny style and mastery of ability have taken you all by storm. I fare stronger than my predecessors. You are neither worthy nor prepared for an adversary such as the world has never seen. Noone (sic) can emulate my style or match my impeccable wits. There is no feeling   like the feeling of speed, the wind through your hair and the sound of crumpling metal, crushing your opponent beneath the wheels.

In my pursuit of perfection I will take myself to new levels bringing you all along willing or unwilling. I go forward while you go back
and somewhere we will meet

Your friend, and admirer

H .

Len paces the Captain's office, clutching the paper and pulling at his thick greasy hair, "Who the hell does this guy think he is? Does he actually think he can outwit me?" lunging toward the desk, "I'm closing in. I'll have him in forty-eight hours."

"You're not the *only* cop on the case. I only assigned you because we need everyone we can on this. Try to stay outside, we don't need you losing it," the captain pauses considerately, "you know, you may want to talk to someone about your anger."

Len whacks the desk, leaning into nose-pore range. "I don't need a goddamn shrink. What I need to do is catch this creep, but I can't... find him. It's like he's everywhere, everywhere and nowhere, in the sky, in the air, in the godforsaken emptiness of the streets. I don't know when I'll catch him, but when I do... I'm going to squeeze, squeeze, SQUE-EZE." Len demonstrates, wringing the air between his hands.

"You're gonna settle the fuck down. We don't need another hothead on the street, there's already a bunch of vigilantes out there."

Len's eyes are growlers hidden below the surface of deep blue.

"And another thing. I told you to finish with the robberies first, but Lamark tells me you've passed it off on him. You need to finish one thing before I give you another."

Len compresses a breath through clenched teeth, throttling the air in front of him as he storms out of the office.

The Captain calls from the doorway, "don't walk out of here, there's a thing or two we have to discuss yet..." a recommendation that Len obligatorily ignores, laying down a patch on his way out of the precinct.

Panic in the heat and exhaust, sweating and restless, driving offensive/ defensive with complete disregard for anyone's safety. Len pulls over in the shade to give himself a pep talk, "Fuck, fuck, fuck, fuck, fuuuuuuck," slamming his fist down on the last *fuck* enabling the horn and shocking pedestrians out of their purposeful stride on the sidewalk next to him. "All this time and what have I got to show for it SQUAT."

Heavy eyes of passing motorists press on him through the glass and steel. He drinks mechanically from a metal canteen and finishes the other half of a submarine sandwich, the first true act of self-preservation in days. Disjointed, fleshy thoughts catch in the gears of his brain. He knows he can't handle much more of this.

He takes another sip, mentally distilling the water into alcohol, soothing, immediate in its effects. Muting thoughts when they become too oppressive. He seeks a liquor store, picking it out amid a jumble of superfluous structures and signs.

He hasn't had so much as a nip since January and wouldn't consider it unless he really needed to forget this car-killer case for a few hours and think of something else. It's down to the Jack Daniels or the Chivas Regal, not much of a choice really, he always chooses scotch over whiskey, but then there's the price to consider and whether he's really going to go through with this or if he's just entertaining the idea before he gets back to catching his man.

Harold is in an adjacent aisle watching Len quibble over the sauce, dilly-dallying between the Jack and the

Chivas, drunk and drunker. From his choice Harold will learn more about Len than Len will ever know about Harold. Whiskey says impulsive, reckless, straight across, perhaps too impulsive to catch the biggest criminal this town has ever seen. Scotch says, slow, patient, attention to detail, not to be underestimated, but maybe too patient. Harold grabs a bottle of tequila and brushes past Len on the way to the till.

Suddenly aggravated and for no apparent reason, Len puts the Jack back on the shelf and grabs the Chivas Regal, then resigned, but still undecided, takes both the Jack and the Chivas.

Harold raises his eyebrows at the sight of both bottles, "how's it goin' friend?"

"Just fine thanks *and you?*" says Len, filtering his contempt through a grin.

"Great. I'm celebrating."

"Celebrating what?"

Harold moves up in line, chatting amiably with the girl behind the counter, taking a little more time perhaps than he needs, stopping on his way out to wave at Len, "see ya' later buddy."

Len looks but doesn't say anything. The girl regards him with a nod. Neither makes an attempt at conversation. In the car, Len opens a bottle of coke, pours half of it out and fills it the rest of the way with scotch. He takes a few sips from the bottle before lurching onto the road. Three spaces away Harold squeezes a lime into his bottle of tequila and shakes salt onto his hand and arm, hitting the car in front of him then shifting into reverse and denting several others before exiting the parking lot. No one seems to witness him.

The streets are deserted save for a few daring pedestrians hurrying home before darkness falls. Len stops at a light. Waiting with all the patience he can muster while an elderly lady drags her cart across the street. She looks at him imploringly, a plea for mercy. He stares back and revs the engine. She wobbles faster. A black Roadmaster idles up beside him. Len looks over at Harold. Harold, eyes glazed over, stares at Len, the only two drivers on the street breathing the same exhaust-laced air adding whatever they do on the exhale. The thought repulses Len. He wants nothing to do with Harold. He has only feelings of contempt for this man he doesn't even know. They go on staring at each other like dogs in parked cars, infuriated by heat and confined space.

The light turns green. Neither moves.

Len examines the car; black with scratch marks on the fenders.

Harold accelerates as Len cogitates.

"Hey," Len screams. Keeping one hand on the wheel as he pulls out his revolver and fires until all the chambers are empty.

"Fuck," he jams four bullets into the tumbler and leans out the window, carefully aiming for one of the rear tires as Harold swerves to play chicken with a slow moving truck.

The truck veers into the adjacent lane on a collision course with Len. Len falls in line behind Harold. The three vehicles pass each other on the wrong side of the road. Len aims and fires, a bullet pierces the gas tank in an explosive one in a million shot. Pieces of metal and burning Naugahyde rain down as he approaches the scene, lips parted and slightly askew. He marvels at how he has driven this maniac to his own demise; a man he thought was pure beast, unresponsive to mortal laws. Fitting, he thinks, all guys like that need is a little push from the right side to drive them completely over the edge. They'd rather take as many people as possible with them than let justice run its course, to come back over to the other side.

He's about to get closer when the shudder-like-shock-wave of a second explosion blows past him. Len goes down in a roll, palms pressed to his eyes. Incendiary figures flutter and flash in blood Rorschach across his field of vision. His hands come away wet, tears, but no blood. Even with his eyes open he still sees it, a voluble figure decocting symmetrically out of the surface viscosity of heat. He unholsters his gun. The pain appears in his hand first, shooting up his arm and down the other side. Contracting his whole body into a fist, opening and closing on command of something outside himself, despite his efforts to bar it. A cold heat forged in some Hadean furnace and tempered in the terrestrial air.

Len curls himself tighter, rolling over and over, until the pain subsides to euphoria, confidence and an inexplicable power. He rises effortlessly and returns to his car. The machine heart that gulps fuel instead of blood throttles in time with his own. He takes one last, long look at the fire reflected in the dark pits of his eyes and drives off.

Night air whistles through open windows. He swerves at the first thing that moves.

150

Marty tells me about this job he got with his uncle on his estate in Norway; forty-grand for four months work, while our regular jobs would only give us a fifth of that in the same amount of time. I tentatively agree, leaving enough room to back out if necessary. What could be so important that we'd have to go out in the middle of nowhere to do some mysterious 'work' for what to me was a small fortune? But Marty assures me it's legit. His uncle had either been employed by or operated one successful business after another, including diamond mining, gold, oil, minerals, even fossils. Buying up all the land in Nunavut he could for next to nothing before the Russians or the Chinese or the Americans could get it.

"He used to tell me, 'there's no reason to beg for a living. You just gotta dress warm'," Marty says.

These are not exactly environmentally-friendly industries, I say, "nothing will ever exist there again, it's poisoned land."

"He doesn't do any of that anymore, this is new technology 'secret stuff' he's working on."

"Like what?"

"I don't know, all he said was there's potential for a new kind of energy using the surplus heat from other processes so nothing is wasted. Something about zero entropy." Marty goes on to tell me that the estate had originally been a Viking settlement, repurposed as an army outpost until it was decommissioned from naval and military service at the end of the World War II, whereupon it reverted to government ownership and was leased to the oil companies.

Norway closed its Northern waterways to rigs and tankers in response to public environmental pressure in the mid-nineties and again the land was abandoned. Norwegian archaeologists, quick to seize upon the lapse in ownership, used the time in limbo to excavate the site, recovering an extensive collection of Viking artifacts for the Oslo museum before the property was sold to a prospector in 1997, who deeming the land too difficult to mine, resold it to Rick; nine thousand acres for nine million in 1999.

"What's with all the nines?"

"He's just an eccentric guy. He never planned it that way, but when those nines started popping up he thought it was a good omen and just went with it, insisting on expanding the territory, paying whatever it took to get nice round numbers 9000, 9 million until the deal went through officially in 1999."

"Yeah, but where did he get the money? Or maybe a better question is, why would he want to use his money to buy useless land that nobody wants."

"It's not useless, it's priceless. It's got mines and ancient Viking settlements."

"Useless, priceless, same thing. If all of a sudden we discovered a bunch of gold, or a diamond meteorite crashed into the Earth, the value of jewelry would go down to about nothing."

"One man's junk is another man's treasure."

Even though I think it's a ridiculous plan, and say as much, I start packing my cold weather gear almost immediately. Rounding it out with some merino and Gore-Tex.

"So, you're in for sure?" says Marty.

"Yeah, just one more question," inserting a rhetorical pause, "is there going to be anyone else there?"

"Who?"

"I don't know, his wife, other workers?"

"Not that I know of. He's pretty secretive about his work, unless he met someone recently, which I don't think he has."

This isn't reassuring, but it doesn't feel like a deal breaker.

"So... you still want to go?"

"Yes, yes. I'll go."

"Good, we fly out tomorrow."

"What if I had said no?"

"He bought the tickets weeks ago, besides, that's not how this one goes."

"What do you mean?"

"Nothing, never mind. You need this, both the money and the experience. I promise. It's like nothing you've ever seen."

The Plane lands in Trondheim, about halfway up country. I look at it on a map, "there's a place called Hell!" I say, grabbing Marty by the arm and pointing at the map.

"Yeah, it just means a shallow cave, you should be happy, it also means lucky."

"What do they call hell then?"

"Helvete."

Marty says that his uncle is coming to pick us up.

"How far is this place?"

"Around a thousand miles."

"Why don't we just fly then?"

"We are."

Marty points out a green and yellow Cessna that has just landed, "that's him."

I wait for people to come out, but no one does. A few moments later the pilot emerges, dressed in a white suit and hat. Marty introduces him officially as Uncle Rick, one of those names that seemed common enough twenty years ago; Richard, Nathan, Robert, William. Big sounding names that get cut down to diminutive versions of themselves, like Dick, Bob, Nate, Will, Rick. Violent, short, obnoxious sounding words, but not as obnoxious as 'Dick'; sharp at first, then gradually flattening like the impact from a blunt object, a lintel or a mantelpiece… rising too high too fast and *bang*.

"I've never taken so many planes in my life," I say.

"That's the only way to travel here," says Rick. "Scandinavia is really just the size of a regular country or continent, but separated by small oceans in between. Very inconvenient for land travel, but nice for flying," he extracts a rolled joint from the inside pocket of his blazer, intoning the sacred wisdom of the sages, 'why drink and drive when you can smoke and fly?'

"What? You're not going to get *high* are you?"

He looks puzzled, as if there were no other way.

I feel a little uneasy as the plane rolls forward, merging with the air currents as we approach a certain speed. The ground falls away and I feel myself split between land and air, mind and body. Occupying that space between. Coming out of the clouds to view the snow-capped peaks of the Børvasstindenes. Each pinnacled dome disguising its height and majesty behind the one in front of it.

Our destination comes into view along a nameless stretch of highland fjord. The only structures visible for miles in any direction and even these are small and squat, looking more like piles of rocks. Marty's uncle takes us in line for an approach over the plot of land before banking steeply into the fjord with only a few hundred feet of clearance on either side.

"Enough planes," I moan through the roaring air.

Marty laughs, "he's just showing off."

We circle the promontory once more, aiming for a narrow strip etched into the berm. Chalk white between pastel fields of lichen. Most of the other promontories are treelined and look pretty rocky, while this one is relatively flat. Surveyed to within a few inches of level.

"He calls this place 'Bardo'," says Marty, "mostly, I think, because it's so remote."

Even though we've landed, I still feel like we're in the air. A mythical kind of place in the clouds, or somewhere outside the orbit of everyday life.

Rick turns to face the direction we just came, "the pink hour," he says. "About as dark as it gets this time of year. In another twenty minutes the sun is going to rise."

From here the land looks a like reptile skin poking above the blanket of snow and ice. Head slumped over the arctic, or antarctic pole. The point where its tail goes into its mouth. Part of a much bigger animal that sleeps for most of its life in order to conserve the energy it must take to move its giant body, or simply because of its age.

It's form only recognizable from above; glaciers capping/ cooling inactive volcanoes and staunching the flow of lava thousands of feet below the surface. The young mountains loaded with precious metals, crystals and other things whose effects on the mind and body cannot be measured, dispelling any notions that I control my emotions here. I wonder if they would make a sound if struck. Waves propagated through faults running beneath my feet. How through this same process they might be moved, or even liquified. The way an earthquake does, but from above rather than below.

The house is built a little ways back from the cliff, incorporating some of the old ruins, covered in mineral graffiti. Abstract sprays of lichen and efflorescence, the wood components long rotted away, leaving the skeletons of structures. Concepts of inside and out dissolved in the salt air.

An excavator has collapsed into a basement near the entrance of one of the buildings. Short, scrubby plants grow in and around terraced gardens, easements carved out of the living rock. Many would-be conquerors had been dashed by volleys of stones thrown from the cliffs above, battered and beaten from their bodies. The survivors living in shallow caves along the promontory until the tides drove them into the mountains.

Rick shows us the area on a geological map. There are mineral deposits, he says; gold, silver, iron, copper, titanium, lead and zinc. Many of the buildings are actually storage areas for ore and raw materials.

Rick changes out of his white suit into a pair of overalls. No movement wasted or misdirected. At times I think he is going to rest, he may in fact mean to, but always picks up another piece of wood or tool and keeps going.

Exhilarating at first, the fatigue of the almost constant daylight begins to suspend the passage of time, suggesting that some border had been crossed. Hours lost track of then recovered, night coming and going like the sun covered up by a cloud. Even the fatigue becomes confused with wakefulness since one cannot be sure of where it came from, or how long it will last. Rick reminds us that we need to sleep, but he never seems to sleep himself. Possibly catching some shut-eye in the workshop when we aren't around before summoning us at some unrecognizable hour with tidings of 'a new day'. He shows us a hole dug into the ground exposing older buildings that had been covered with centuries of debris. "The foundations are still good. They just need new roofs and floors. A good foundation never deteriorates. You can keep adding onto it. No one knows who actually built them or how old they really are."

Some of the foundations end suddenly in terraces at the edge of the cliff as if, over time, erosion had brought down whole sections at once, revealing the layers of occupation from nomadic hunter/ gatherers to seafaring Norse. Floors stacked upon floors with bones, potsherds and primitive weapons. A sheet of dirt slides down revealing the smooth side of a squared stone. I work around the object a little more, revealing one of its edges, then a corner. Whatever it is, it's big.

"Hey, I think I found something."

"Good job," says Rick. "That's what I've been looking for, the cornerstone. Now we can rebuild the wall." Building wood forms onto the ancient remnants of walls and pouring in concrete, then pulling the wood out from the hardened concrete to prepare more forms. The work continues at a pace I wouldn't have thought possible and I don't even seem to get tired, working as the day is long, which turns out to be not only all day, but all night. I don't even remember the last time we ate. I tell Marty who tells Rick that we need something to eat. Rick goes away briefly and returns with a pot of stew, steaks and boiled potatoes regaling us over dinner with his increasingly frequent anecdotes; an incident that occurred back in his days of the Siberian war. His voice like a close shave in the brisk air; the only sound besides the grating of our shovels in the frigid earth. Perhaps it's got something to do with his teeth; diamond crowns beaming rays of light before disappearing into the dark maw of his mouth.

He explains how, when the guns' mechanisms froze, the soldiers had to use ice, stabbing each other with icicles or freezing their shit in the snow. How he had known a man who, in the process of freezing to death, chewed off his own lips thinking that he was eating fresh meat. He assures us that unlike what you see in the movies, hungry men have no reservations about eating each other. As if the instinct had been stored in our bodies all this time and under the right conditions thaws out and becomes part of our nature. "Men were prone to devouring the flesh of their comrades. No one talked about it because no one knew who was next. After a while all references to food were code for their own flesh."

For a moment I feel as if I'm there; the feeling of being one with the land, instinct rising to a drive for survival and steeply dropping off to no desire at all. Eating another person's flesh not as a person, but as the world. The way I imagine an animal might feel; as much a part of me as I am of it. No needs, no wants, no desires, just the oneness with the mountains, the snow and the wind in my ears.

The story ends or is interrupted and I find myself back in the present, place. The pause in the music where I notice the silence rather than the sound. Marty and I poke idly at the ground with our shovels, as if loosening our voices from the Earth. Voluble thoughts warmed under consciousness crack at the surface of speech, sheets of ice disguising the depths beneath. Not words exactly, but some semblance of meaning is exchanged, from a solid to a gas, reconstituted as a liquid and frozen and thawed and frozen again.

"I'm most at home in the arctic," he continues, "I've sought out work and made fortunes in Canada, Scandinavia, Greenland and Siberia. The customs of the people of the north fascinate me. I respect their will to survive. They haven't had it easy, no coconut palms and grass skirts for them. They are an intensely spiritual people with almost no concept of war. Populations being so small and the land so vast, they rarely come into contact with one another and when they do the company is often welcomed. Exchanging stories, members, descriptions of lands far away. Inuit women are the most beautiful of all God's creatures and I have had the pleasure of knowing a few of them in my life. During the winter nights they dance under the aurora borealis, skin and hair adorned with ice crystals. The lights come so close that they wear them as make-up; exotic colours that cannot be found anywhere else on Earth. Their courtship rituals, like all aspects of arctic life, are particularly intense. In competition for potential mates, the men will engage in staring contests to melt ice. They focus their gaze on blocks of ice for days, weeks in some cases, until they are completely melted. The melting of ice is considered a virtue, a magical feat likened to the miracle of birth and rebirth and associated with the onset of spring, fertility and growth. Where we might sleep with a warm stone in winter, Inuit boys and girls are brought up to sleep with blocks of ice, the one who melts it the fastest is said to be the most passionate lover, the most desired for a bedmate. Many single men and women freeze on account of not having a bedmate. To the uninitiated the arctic can be a very unforgiving place. That's why they undergo such rigorous trials. One does not last long on his own. The shamans of the Inuit are the most amazing of all. Some of their feats are nothing less than miraculous. I have seen them cure the sick with a flame passed over the body and cut it open with a ceremonial blade of ice to extract a red devil. If someone commits a capital crime, such as murder, they themselves are not killed, but ostracized from the village, a punishment far worse than death."

Rick picks up a shovel and continues to dig out the foundation of a building, while Marty and I rebuild the walls, getting them ready for a new roof.

When we're alone I ask Marty about the cannibal story and the ice melting, "do you think he's been out here a little too long? Isolation does a lot to one's sense of objectivity."

"Maybe a little, but he's been saying this stuff for years. He'd be gone for a long time and come back with a bunch of stories like that. I've heard 'em all before."

"How 'bout those grillz, eh?" I say.

"They're something alright."

"They can't be real though."

"Oh yeah, I've seen him tear the lids off cans and pull nails out of boards."

"I'm surprised he doesn't have a bionic hand."

"Not yet, he's a little reluctant to go 'borg. He says he'll give them a few more years to get the bugs out."

I feel as if I were once again, part of the environment. I only have to look at the mountains to imagine I'm there. Flying or else standing on a distant peak, the light shining through me at an angle, just a shimmer in the air, almost invisible.

Our work is methodical, bringing us in and out of consciousness. I barely notice what I'm doing. We have three out of four of the walls built when I notice a voice in my head that isn't mine. Rick is behind us, holding a couple of joists that are meant to support the roof.

"There are virtually no ruins in the arctic, although we know they exist; monolithic ice sculptures carved out of solid blocks of ice that over the years have been intermingled with the natural formations, melted and refrozen to make smooth surfaces. Delicate arches, grand canyons, hoodoos, stalactites and stalagmites of ice. Columns of atlas, pillars of Hercules, holding up the world that they also depend from. Things are temporary here, built for now. The poles shift, glaciers encroach and retreat, the people do likewise, using the exposed land as a corridor, a way through. Ice is a transitory state. It facilitates movement. The people who live with the ice are the most adaptable and resilient of earth's inhabitants and will probably survive the longest. While we drown in floods or succumb to fire, the people of the ice have survived, some have even been reanimated after being frozen for some twenty thousand years, yes. The Earth is destined to repeat the cycles of birth and rebirth through fire, water, ice and so on, but it is the ice people who always survive."

The list of the uncle's occupations and achievements goes on as if he had lived several lifetimes. He raises a hand, dirty and matted like a bear's paw. Platinum rings inset with diamonds—more diamond than metal—twinkle in the light that strikes them.

"Diamonds don't have to be mined anymore, they can be grown, under controlled conditions of heat and pressure." Simulating the process with a rock squeezed between his hands. "We're talking 4000 degrees centigrade, with pressures of 1000 pounds per square inch. The greater the pressure the faster the diamonds grow. One day diamonds will be as plentiful as glass or steel, a glittery cityscape of walls, wheels, doors and manhole covers all constructed entirely of densely interwoven carbon atoms." The rock having fulfilled its purpose of being turned into diamond is tossed to the ground, unchanged. "The atoms in both carbon and diamond are bound in covalent bonds, but with coal and graphite fewer bonds are made between the atoms giving carbon-based life its plasticity."

Despite his solitary existence, Rick is surprisingly utopian in his vision, or perhaps not so surprising, now that I've had a chance to get to know him. A deep-thinking idealist come all the way out here to do his kind of thinking and not just thinking, but building. Building what, I don't know. Not an ice machine, the world has plenty of that, unless he's planning to cool the planet.

He says whatever it is it'll revolutionize the way we think about nature. "The Earth's crust tells a complete story, our part however will not be in stone like the rest of history, but an oily plastic film, a sludge that never fully solidifies. Does that remind you of anything, like maybe we've been here before? It's black, oily involvement in our lives. I'mean where the *hell* is this stuff *still* coming from? We're talking about a-hundred-million-year-old technology. Dino' died so we could drive cars? *I don't think so.* That's not pseudoscience. That's preposterous." His frequent anachronisms like arcane references, perhaps too arcane to exist outside his head. "Oil's no damn good for anything, except death, dug up and spit out with the potential to kill again, or, if you want to put it in a more… *scientific* way, consider the law of conservation of energy." His brows ascending the steppes of his forehead, "that's a *hell of a lot* of energy. Hundreds of millions of years of death and decay, and who knows what kind of spiritual load it's bringing with it. Like *what if that's not what it's for, folks.* The planet using it the same way a machine does, to facilitate the movement of parts. Its removal making earthquakes more of a pang; a pain, like pushing a steak through the colon without digesting it first. The earth…" He slams his spade into the ground, steam rising from the fresh gouge, "can provide all the energy we need. A truly planetary civilization must some day harness the power in the Earth as a step toward leaving it."

The sun hovers low on the horizon only to bounce back up into another day.

"I've got a solution for the melting of polar ice caps… it's a kind of carbon I call Carbon 9 or Carbonine, similar to Carbonate, haha, get it? Actually, it's not really carbon at all, but a nanobot that can turn any atom into diamond and I'm not talking Cubit Zychonia, this is the real thing. I call 'em Pokemon, ya' know, because they spread like crazy."

Marty looks a little lost, like he is still trying to comprehend how any of this is possible, or how it even came up to begin with. Although it sounds like a joke, I get the feeling that it might be more real than any of us think. Imagining the Conde mountain tops, Transvaal glaciers, DeBeers lakes and Incomparable peaks forcing nature to amend its laws in order to overcome this new threat. Of course, these are just the paranoid thoughts of an over-stimulated and sleep deprived brain. Who knows what's really happening on those mountains, a combination of angles of light and sunsets that go on for hours.

"Diamonds change colour depending on what kind of minerals are in the ore when it is crushed; red is iron, yellow is nitrogen, blue... is boron, and green is uranium or some other radioactive material," Rick lights a joint, vapours rising in the clear air as we pass it back and forth.

An owl flies out of one of the old, stone buildings.

"Wow, I guess that guy can't sleep either," I say. "A hoot owl."

I feel tired for the first time in a while, so tired that I want to lay down, "it's getting cold, I have to go inside," though despite being exhausted, I'm unable to sleep. Too quiet, too bright with no point of reference, like floating in clear air. I tear the sleeve off my shirt and tie it around my head as a blindfold. *Finally,* I think. *Why didn't I think of this before?*

It's afternoon when I wake up, but there's no way to tell. Light the colour of lemonade; a few sips of opalescent fluid in the glass, spirits rising, in gradual evaporation.

I find Rick outside, mudding the walls of the building we had been working on yesterday. The joists are in place, just waiting on the cross beams and the shakes that get put on last. He says he needs me to go into the workshop and finish planning the boards. There's a pile of milled lumber in the corner. I see Rick on a scaffold above, angling poles and pieces of rebar. He eyes me as a piece of rebar comes crashing through the ceiling. It hits me, but I don't feel it. The concussion throwing drifts of dust into the air. Seconds pass, then minutes. *I must be in shock,* I think. I'm gonna need immediate medical attention at least.

There's only one exit, which is also the entrance and it's locked. I don't feel any pain so I think I must really be in trouble, inspecting myself, making sure everything's still there, or that I don't have something extra, like a ten-foot piece of rebar sticking out of my back.

Rick opens the door, stirring up a few centuries of dust and debris. He looks around, picking up a hammer as if he was looking for it everywhere, and throws it full force at my head. I don't have time to duck before it hits me, registering only as a distant thud. I reel back, gazing out of the hole in my head like looking through the wrong end of a pair of binoculars. I touch my face. No blood. I pick up the hammer and throw it back. It hits him in the head and bounces off the wall behind. There seems to be an in exhaustible supply of hammers, chisels, saws, knives, wrenches and pneumatic drills at our disposal. We brush off blow after blow, most of them potentially fatal, which is one advantage of being already dead. My next throw slicing through the empty space where his body had been. Alone now, I announce my intention to return to my body, to wake up. Expecting to see myself lying on the floor, but I don't. Instead, I see myself, as myself, albeit a little lighter. Moving like breathing, all I have to do is pump a little air through my body, if it *is* a body, and float where I want to go. Through the door and into the cold arctic air.

The world is quiet, just the sound of freezing and refreezing ground, creaking and grinding in a constant settling motion. My body the same temperature inside as out, not frozen, just numb, water as cold as blood.

I stare across the fjord, willing myself across, scaling rocks at the peaks, drifts of snow in the valleys, at home in every inch of space.

Aura borealis bleeding outside the lines. Insects fly through my translucent skull like thoughts scattered incomplete, never quite growing into ideas.

Clouds settle, siphoning moisture through a network of channels, only a few feet of shoreline visible at a time. I turn around and start back, spacing breaths to modulate speed and altitude; long-deep ones, or short-close ones, skimming the tops of waves; a breeze entering familiar ranges.

The shore is littered with wood and debris, weather beaten boards of boathouses and platforms dragged away with the sea. Some of the caves in the cliff face have been filled. I drift into a chamber hung with stalagmites. Rotted wood platforms support the rusted iron tracks of a trolley line. Boxes of dynamite sit in piles on the floor, some of it soaked by the tides, turning the ground around it black.

A narrow shaft rises to the surface. I float up through a wooden door, entering on the cool cellar of the house. Polyethylene walls flap in the breeze so it appears that the house is floating. The work continuing where our lives left off. I glide over freshly poured concrete. Wires and empty light bulb fixtures dangle from the ceiling.

I focus energy against the wall to see what it will do, only a disembodied thud. The house seems to achieve a greater sense of completion as I drift through. Organized non-domestically, with its own sense of order and tidiness. Doors lead to wings in each of the cardinal directions. I take the door on my left, entering on what could be a living room, cluttered with half-finished wood projects, various taxidermy, a few armchairs with the stuffing coming out. I hear footsteps on the floor above, voices, including a woman's.

I take a breath and rise through the floor into another, larger room, hiding behind a curtain like Hamlet's ghost, just in case they can see me, which I have a feeling they can.

A few seconds later a girl emerges from an adjacent room, long blonde hair flowing around her face and the outer curves of breasts swaying like ballasts beneath a silk robe, open on either side.

She sees me through the curtain. Raising her arm and then a finger. I feel myself pulled towards her. I don't know how long it's been, without a body to touch.

She presents herself in the form of a pop star, someone she identifies with strongly. I want to embrace her, to know a real connection, but she says we can only be friends. It's her punishment, having dodged love all her life. She says that love was there all along.

she just didn't want to accept it, not that she wasn't ready. She had the chance many times, but passed it up in favour of what she could get just because she could, until finally it had its way with her. "I had a spirit but it never fully developed because I never needed it." This is her only regret, she says, that she didn't know this before and now that she does, she doesn't have a body anymore. "It's torture," she says "to appreciate one's life and body, but have neither. Love isn't always a good thing, it can destroy a friendship. Love joins people spiritually, sex joins them physically, but friendship *as* friendship always stays the same. There's always this distance between us so that virtue and distance essentially mean the same thing." She speaks slow and thoughtfully, as if fending off a word that might compromise the message and strip it of meaning.

I say I'm not sure if I want to be friends.

Her form flickers and dematerializes as if she cannot exist and think at the same time. She says it's me that threatens to strip her words of meaning, that I should not objectify her or think of her in any way or she will disappear.

I ask her about her relationship with the Uncle.

She says it is her punishment to live an unfulfilled life until she has worked off this burden of the flesh completely.

I try, but cannot avoid looking at her as she begins to disappear before my eyes. After she's gone I continue on my way, my purpose the only thing keeping me from floating away completely. All a soul knows is how to make a plan and follow it through so they can rest.

In life one fears others and God, but in death all that matters is vengeance and rest.

A long exhalation propels me into the bedroom. Uncle sits passively at the edge of the bed as if resigned to his fate, but I know it must be a ploy, he too has a plan and won't go down without a fight.

Usually, it's the one who *enters* a room that is at a disadvantage, and this is no exception. I wait for another barrage of objects, an arsenal of weaponry pulled out from under the bed and between the sheets, but instead he speaks with what sounds like genuine contrition, "you slept here. Where I am now. There were posters on the walls then, of bands and those Betty Boob girls. I was jealous of you and your youth. You were better than us. People only liked us because we threw big parties. We were rich and arrogant. Anyone who saw us knew that, but we had a presence that displaced others and that counts for a lot."

"Where's Marty?" I ask

"I had to let him go."

I shudder involuntarily, there is no disguising my feelings, they are all I have. Surrounding me in various shades of orange, red and violet.

Without speaking, Rick gets up and passes through a wall. He wants me to find him somewhere in this house, or he wants to find me.

The western sky now a cold blue, unable to rise out of its bed, the result of having kept itself awake for so long. Its creaking voice the sound of a giant bird. Tenebrous feathers scraping the peaks and boulders that crowd out the winter sky.

Rick stands behind a turntable and mic. He reaches down, I assume to pick up some kind of weapon or object to throw at me, but instead he flicks a switch. Multiple turntables turn on at once, all at the end of the record. Hitting the edge of the flat disc and bouncing back.

"I was just getting ready for a broadcast," he says.

"What are you doing with all these," I say pointing to the record players.

"The needle plays in the grove and amplifies the sound through a diamond tip."

"I understand how they work."

He has an extensive record collection, including of course diamond records.

"A diamond record is an album that has sold 10 million copies. Soon all of my albums will be diamond."

Shadows fill out the proportions of our bodies so we look almost like ourselves again, though without the solidity of flesh.

Rick picks up the needle from one of the record players and turns the record over, setting the needle back down at the beginning.

A slow jazz tune warbles through the speaker, the hard medium reflecting the sound rather than projecting it so it's like a whisper of itself. Drawing something out of the stone to occupy the room.

Apparitions, ghosts, spectral projections converge from all over the world and presumably time. Some taking a little longer than others, depending on how far they have come, dressed in everything from banyans to bikinis doing things they only wished they could do when they were alive.

One last dance before they depart forever, this time to I don't know where.

Everything is diamond of course, diamond tiara, diamond necklace, diamond earrings even the glasses. Guests tipping champagne out of diamond goblets into puddles on the floor.

Rick starts turning all the records over, assembling a kind of Pavlovian set of familiar tunes which gets the old folks moving 'the way we used to do' like a return trip, disappearing back the way they came, memory lane or some such place; 'The Land of the Dead', like a suburban street that keeps looping back on itself on some sunny summer day. The trick is not to get stuck at any point, to be as fluid as a record in a grove that when it ends all you have to do is turn it over. No tape to unwind, no film to cut. Jumping from one part of the grid to another so we can be anywhere we want at any time.

It's starting to happen, the room has gotten colder, the air dried out, to clearer than clear. The walls turning opaque, admitting a yellowish glow.

Slabs of smoky diamond spread in the grout between the tiles, up the walls and over marble countertops. Changing their molecular structure right before my eyes; octahedral, irradiated, deformed in every shade and hue. Storing the light from the sun that is now about to set for the remainder of the year.

Rick has one last surprise for us. He lights a wick that burns through the floor.

The house rocks, but not from the music.

The blast sends us up and out through the trees, valleys and fjords. Air currents carried overland, the cumulus of a mother hurricane settling in over the Eastern seaboard, coast of Massachusetts, Michigan, the shores of Lake Superior, like an inland ocean glowing pink, red and orange at the break of day.

Looking down at the places I knew. Knowing that it won't last long. There is no rest for the wind. The particles it carries can only stay together for so long before they settle to the ground.

But what I thought was me is not. There are no parts. Everything is interacting and being interacted with. I am not a body, just a pair of eyes and not even that, just an awareness, preserved part from memory and part from what I can still feel. Making of it one place. The place I am in.

The Book of John pt.1, 'The Curse of John'

John responded to an ad for a singer/ songwriter that we happened to put up in the music store where he worked. He sent us a CD with him playing 'Interstate Love Song' and an original called 'Soul Cry'. Our stereotypically longhaired, bass player, Dylan Wayne DeHavelyn, who weighed about 260 pounds and always wore shorts (even in the winter), liked it because Stone Temple Pilots are his favorite band. John was the first and only guy we auditioned. I knew we should have kept looking but Dylan didn't like looking for band members and reasoned that since John worked at a music store he could get us good deals.

"Who cares about deals if he sucks?" I say.

"He's as good as anyone we might find," says Dylan. *"Can't you hear my soul cryin' tonight...* are you kidding? Anyone can write better lyrics than that."

We had a name for our band, *Fuel for Fire*, but it doesn't matter because we didn't play any shows. I never told him straight out that I didn't like his songs. Sometimes telling people what you don't like about them does more harm than good and with stuff as bleak and sentimental as *Soul Cry*, I was almost certain he couldn't do any better anyways. So, I buried my true feelings behind drumbeats and became a friend to the guy, who away from the mic wasn't so bad.

John does cocaine on occasion, a combination of powdered and crack, something that occurs to him after a few drinks. He says *I could use a line right now* and repeats it until he gets one, a true eighties man, or eighties child at least. His daddy probably listened to a lot of Hughie Lewis, maybe worked at the local bank. I'm almost positive on this, I remember some conversation to the purpose. One night in particular comes to mind. Sometime in summer, 2000, muddied by drinks spread out over several hours and bars, culminating in a trip to a bathroom deep inside the penetralia of some building or complex of buildings designed to meet a standard, but not exceed it. A one stall hole in the wall with mirror and sink, though all I really remember is the countertop, dully reflecting the harsh white glare of fluorescents as I metabolized my first ever line of cocaine. The place turned out to be Fast Eddie's, a Mediterranean restaurant off the Island Highway on the way out of town (no matter which way you're headed, everybody who comes to Nanaimo is always on their way out of town). I had no recollection of how we got there. John had to remind me what happened. The last thing I remembered was drinking at the Queens. More than I could afford, which meant that John had bought us a few pitchers and then of course he needed a line so here we were. After locating myself in the mirror I pondered my unfamiliar surroundings. The mode by which we had arrived and the action of the drug seemed consistent with an abduction type scenario; missing time followed by a revelation similar to the removal of a blindfold, as if I were crossing over into another world, the dark *underworld* of the Nanaimo drug scene.

"It sobers you up," he said.

We had a few more drinks with appies until the bartender began to look at us funny. John paid our bill and we walked the three blocks to his apartment to do more lines.

Over the course of the day and days that followed, I began to notice the shadow side. The fiends, night-crawlers and addicts emerging, unbidden, from the throw of streetlights and alleyways to accost passersby in short terse conversations before switching to the subject of drugs. As if drugs were an impulse buy and I would somehow become intrigued by their convincing sales pitch. "Nice night isn't it? Would you like to buy some crack?"

Their faces already registering a reaction to something I hadn't yet said. Thinking five moves ahead to what's in my pocket, what they might be able to get for it, their next score, meal, customer. Presenting your average law-abiding citizen with a new kind of danger to which there is no easy way out. Politeness only encourages them, while rudeness may provoke a fight, so the best thing to do is blend in, which brings up a host of other issues; the perverse reversal of destiny, sending emissaries that instead of trying to save my soul, were bent on dissolving it over a series of sleepless nights and drained mornings with all the colour washed out.

Why of all things did arbitrary chance seek to engage me through hookers and drug dealers rather than a solicitous helper, a benevolent friend? Was it to do with some Mephistophelian death deal made during that interval (crack) between worlds, loosing *beings* who from then on would pursue me through nighttime and now daytime streets?

John kept at it long after I found the self-respect to quit. His problem, I think, was that he never learned from his experiences because he didn't seem to suffer any consequences. He'd lose money and his mom would just send more, not that she was really trying to help or teach him any lessons, but because money wasn't an issue and she equates money with unconditional love. I don't know. I don't know the woman. Maybe he tells her he's undergone some significant change and has learned from his mistakes. The level of responsibility John maintains illustrated by the fact that he has an illegitimate son in Nanaimo that he never sees.

During the time of our association I witnessed several interesting scenes and fabricated a few more, including; 'The Curse of John'; 'Fast Eddies John' and 'Inadvertently-Soliciting-Prostitution John'.

To begin with, the just plain old John, before he became the subject of fictional accounts, was only in the band for a few months before he got into an argument about song writing with Dylan and our other guitarist Marty. We were in the middle of playing one of John's songs. Marty, our lead guitarist, was doing an unconventional solo, where he'd drag an Allen key, or any kind of thin metal bar really, over the strings and strum a fast pattern. John carried on for a few more bars after the solo and stopped in mid-chorus. "Okay. That was shit."

"Why?" I said.

"It sounded like a bunch of noise," addressing Marty, "what kind of solo was that?"

"It's called an 'Allen key solo'," says Marty.

"How is that a solo, or a melodic progression of any kind?"

"It just is."

"It's too obscure for this project, just play..." John diddles out a twangy little solo.

Marty mimics it with an exaggerated bend of the strings, "do you mean play any number of redundant and outdated rock guitar solos? Or maybe something that sounds a little too much like someone else?"

John's face turns red. I know Marty doesn't give a damn what John thinks. If John says that Marty's playing sounds like noise it's more of a complement than an insult. Marty and I have been in plenty of bands. We know what we're doing. We're only here because of each other, if he goes, I go and vice versa.

John shifts his attention to Dylan "and you should stop playing your bass like a guitar."

Dylan snaps back, "why don't you concentrate on how you play and not worry about anyone else."

"Because these are *my* songs."

"Yeah, and all your songs sound the same."

"That's *because* they have *structure*. No one goes to a show to see the bass player wank off."

"Well, why don't you write another three chords about it, *Rockstar*." The instrument making a deep, meaty sound as it strikes the side of his leg, sending a low-end shudder through the room. John hadn't seen this side of Dylan yet and now, with the bass rig still humming through every live mic in the room, Dylan, also known as Black Thorn, had just gone into dungeon master mode and was waiting for John to make his move.

Marty and I look at each other, all we could do was sit and watch the inevitable dissolution of the band that neither of us really liked anyway. While they finalized the break up by saying a few more terrible things to each other, I went to the rec room to do butterfly presses and avoid the brewing hostility. No one was complaining about me. I was friends with all of them and the songs were too easy for me to screw up.

Although we never jammed together again, this was just the beginning of our association. John, having signed the contract for the jam space we were occupying, got hold of the remaining money and went back to Alberta after spending it on drugs. While John was in Alberta, Marty and his fiancé, Carla, were breaking up. She began talking to John on MSN messenger and they decided, without consulting Marty, that John should move in with them. Within a week, John had his old job back and was sleeping with Carla in her and Marty's old bedroom, while Marty slept on the couch like a castaway on a friend ship lost in a lover's Bermuda triangle. I was having roommate issues of my own at the time, so I couldn't offer him a place to stay. During their month-long cohabitation, Marty lived in tight vectors between the university, liquor store and the woods around the apartment. Luckily it was May, so he could spend as much time outside as possible. He wasn't despondent, just tired and hungry, living as he did pretty much like a hobo, except he had a couch to sleep on. Whatever he and Carla used to do and then what John and Carla did, he came to hate; the music, the people, the places, even the food. Eating was becoming a problem. He couldn't afford to eat out all the time and when he came 'home' he had to smell what they'd eaten and it would made him sick. They'd ask if he wanted the leftovers, to which he'd invariably say no and then eat them anyway, along with whatever else they had in the house. Stealing was okay, but accepting charity or a friendly gesture was not.

In June John and Carla got a place across the street and Marty floated for a bit. Living while he could in rented rooms, jam spaces and friend's couches, playing parties to sleep on the floor, etc. There was no news from the 'twits', Marty's collective name for John and Carla, until around September when we got a big update.

A few months into his arrangement with Carla, John financed a guitar from work and left to see his folks in Alberta, when he returned a few weeks later, Max, the owner, refused to give him his job back because he was behind on the payments and generally unreliable. John said he'd already paid and wouldn't pay any more. The altercation moved to the back entrance where Max threw him down a flight of stairs.

Marty heard the news and applied for the job, anticipating that John would come around and maybe he, Marty, could throw him down the stairs too, but when John found out that Marty had taken his job, he tried to tell everyone how Marty had been abusive towards Carla. How he'd stepped in and threw him out of the house.

No one believed him of course and Marty vowed to get revenge.

John's doing good for John these days, Johnny B. Goode, he woke up at nine-thirty thinking that no one could possibly do a better job of being John than him. People tell John he can't do things, but John says he can. He's the kind of guy that won't let what he can't do stand in his way. He doesn't believe it when they tell him he's no good, though usually it's behind his back. He may be someone you know, the guy you're dating, have dated, will date; always looking for an upgrade, an addition to his prolific list of stats.

The remnants of John's breakfast slides into the big plastic garbage bag atop gobs of waxed paper, parchment and plastic. No compost, no recycling, nothing that looks like an organic vegetable.

It's Carla's day off from the café. She's wearing her robe, hair in disarray, gazing at John as he meanders through an even more simplified rendition of Nickleback's, "How You Remind Me," singing with conviction, *a-and this is h-how, you-ou re-mind meee.*

"I love that song. Did you play it for me?"

"Of course. Did I wake you up?"

"I love to wake up to the sound of your guitar."

They kiss with the guitar still resonating between them.

"Check this one out. I've been working on it for the last few days," playing three bars of a power ballad before starting in on the words.

You make me feel like I am real. I can't stop thinking about the way. I wake up beside you everyday. You know I'm here to stay. I start to sing. I'd never trade that for—anything your face is love and I'm in love

"That's beautiful, is that for me?"

"Of course it is baby. I love you."

They kiss again, Carla falling sideways onto his lap.

"No, no, you're going to crush the guitar."

Carla gets up, pouting, "what, is the guitar more important than me?"

"Of course not, but how am I supposed to write songs as beautiful as you without it?"

"That's so *sweet*," one of only a few words that those truly in love can use in all sincerity without hearing what it sounds like to others.

"I'd love to stay here with you all day, but I gotta go to the gym."

"Miss me," she says.

"Me too."

John gets in the car, John goes to the bar, John plays the guitar.

Last week he was benching 220 pounds, today he plans on boosting it up to 240. Sweat is excreted. Adrenaline floodgates open and mix with blood. He inhales as he lifts and exhales easing the weights back down. "And this is how you remind me..." but he's not thinking of Carla now.

A busty, well-sculpted blonde is working out on a rowing machine in front of him. He continues, hoping she will notice his effort and skill, "nine... ten," finishing his set and sitting the next one out. The girl wipes her head with a hand towel and leaves without looking in his direction.

John does another rep and toddles off after her. Just long enough for it to be considered following and not a legitimate attempt at establishing contact, scanning the vending machines, water fountain and other loci of break time congregation, making a show of looking disinterested.

After a few minutes he feels it in the plumbing and ducks into the men's room. He can't resist taking a look in the mirror, searching for signs of improvement, proof that hard work pays off, if not at work than at least when he plays.

At the cafeteria he orders chicken on rye with salad. He usually refuses vegetables unless they're indistinguishable beneath sauce or dressing, but there's a sign above the counter that says, 'you are what you eat,' and in small print 'size matters, eat salad instead of fries.' John makes a mental note to eat more vegetables.

On his way back he sees the blonde sipping from the fountain by the door. *Wait till she gets a load of me,* he thinks, sucking in his gut and pushing out his chest.

The words leave his mouth before he has a chance to think, "I saw you working out. Those are great abs, not to mention buns. We should get together some time and do a *real* work out." While most people might glance at a girl, entertain some thoughts, maybe say something lame or even heartfelt, John just does what comes natural. That's what the tapes tell him to do. *Be active instead of passive. Don't over think it. Don't be afraid to say what's on your mind.*

"Um, I don't think so. Instead of working on your pecs maybe you should work on your approach."

John remains stoic despite the hasty rejection. *She just doesn't know me well enough. She doesn't know what she wants.* He isn't desperate or even looking to have an illicit encounter. He merely likes to be seen as sexy and wanted by every girl.

John finishes with a cool down on the treadmill and heads to work. His role in society is crucial; he is bringing food to the people. Sometimes they give him tips.

It's eight pm, near the end of his shift and he's looking forward to settling down on the couch with Carla to watch a movie, make out and have sex before the movie is over. Navigating the streets from memory, he's got five minutes to find the house and give the people what they want, otherwise it's free. There aren't many places in town he can't find. He does his little sprint to the door, straightens his red hat and coat and rings the bell. Ten seconds. He's about to ring again when the door opens, revealing, by degrees, half a face, a shoulder, then a firm, perky breast. The door angling inward until it is in its fully open position, "*hiiii*, can I help you?"

"You ordered a pizza?"

"Yes, come in," smiling, it seems, genuinely.

John enters and stands erect.

She's got a fan of blue and purple bills and is brushing them lightly across her chest, "go on put down those heavy pizzas. Don't you want to touch me?"

John plops the pizzas down on the counter. The girl puts the money on top of the boxes and unbuttons her pants, rolling them down around her ankles, then peels off her underwear and strolls up to John, breasts brushing his red delivery coat. John swells like a hotdog in a rotisserie.

"Whoa, hey. I'm John."

"Shut up and kiss me."

John dispenses with the formalities and proceeds to roll his tongue around in the stranger's mouth.

"Check it out, I've got the perfect prank to get even with John," says Marty.

Marty and I are sitting on a bench in the park behind my house smoking a joint.

An expectorating silence settles, "I'm listening."

"Say, for instance, I tell an escort to go to your house, while we phone in a fake pizza order. Say John goes to the door and presents her with a steaming hot pizza... she's half naked and says, for example," Marty affecting a higher feminine tone, "oh, come in. I've got the money for ya' honey." Marty executes a kind of 'sexy dance' with the pretend money, waving it in front of his chest.

"Ha ha. That's funny... but why would we do that?"

"Do you think he'd be able to say no? He'll get fired for sure and Carla will know that he'd been with another chick."

"Do you know how much that would cost!?"

"I'll pay. Besides it couldn't be more than a couple hundred dollars. It'll be perfect because he doesn't know where you live."

"Yeah, but that's like an ounce and a half," I protest, economically.

"This is going to be better than any weed man. I'll have her leave the blinds open so we can take pictures... to show Carla."

"Oh, you mean like a P.I., or a peeping Tom, or what?"

"No. For *revenge*."

"Ooooh, ahh."

"Good. Give me your cell phone," says Marty, snatching the phone from my hand. He calls and arranges a meeting with the escort at my house.

"OK, it's all done. They estimated about four-hundred dollars for the time we need and the required action."

"That was fast."

"I called earlier I just needed to confirm the time. John will be starting work about now," says Marty consulting his watch, making silent cerebral calculations. "Can you spot me a hundred and fifty bucks?"

Incredulously, "no, I can't *give you* a hundred and fifty dollars."

"C'mon I'll pay you back."

"What do you have in the way of proof that your plan will even work? What if he doesn't like this girl, what if he says no. Ever think of that?"

"Uh... *no*. That would never happen. John'll always go for the easy lay, no matter what. Especially if it's what he thinks is an ideal situation. Which it is, as long as he doesn't suspect some kind of trick, he'll most definitely go along with it. He'll never chose duty over pleasure. He's like an over-stimulated rat," making mouse masticating sounds. "Besides this isn't some cheap Haliburton ho, we're taking about. She's a student."

"Did you see her?"

"I saw her photo online, she's good."

"Right, doctored photo."

"She's an actress. It's a promo shot. Anyway, I inquired over a week ago. I've put a lot of planning into this and I've got the money, just not all of it, all I need is to use your place."

"You've been planning it all week and yet you wait until now to tell me?"

"I'm getting to it alright. It's complex. The main thing is time. The more time he spends in the house the later he is with the rest of the orders. All we need is fifteen minutes. Then it's free right? So first I call in. I make a big scene with all kinds of substitutions. I ask about where they source their cheese. Is it gluten free? No. Well can I get whole wheat? No. Fine, then I make it seem like I'm going to have a fit if it's late like,

I WANT MY PIZZA HOT AND IF ITS NOT HERE IN FIFTEEN MINUTES I WON'T PAY. Then we'll run back up here and watch through these binoculars." He pulls a pair of binoculars out of his jacket.

"Oh boy. What happened to taking pictures?"

"Well, yeah. That too," pulling a black nylon case out of his overstuffed hobos backpack. "I got it from some fiend downtown. I think it's a good one."

It's an expensive-looking camera and likely has a pretty heavy karmic load coming along with it as well, not to mention whatever pictures are on it. "Hmm," shrugging off any apparent interest or concern.

Affronted, Marty tries to promote the idea that this is a fun thing to do and not just a stab at his ex and her new beau, "something we can look back on in fifteen years and more importantly it's something we can do together, as buds. Besides afterwards we get pizza and beer," as if this gesture of machismo solidarity will serve to convince me. "I can't believe you *don't* want to do this."

We're outside the house smoking a joint when the girl arrives in a taxi. Pretty, brunette, about twenty years old. She strolls up and introduces herself as Brandy.

"Hi. I'm Marty, and this is Dave," offering her the spent roach.

"No thanks," says Brandy.

Not a good way to start things off.

"Sorry," I say, snatching the roach out of Marty's hand. "We've got more if you want."

Marty blinks and flashes me a quick, but perceptible, what do I do now? Realizing that after planning the whole thing, he doesn't know what to say to this girl whom I can actually feel go cold from three feet away.

"C'mon in the house," he offers.

"It's okay," I say. "We'll explain inside."

Brandy glances inquisitively around the clean, but empty kitchen/foyer, "well, I don't know what you guys have in mind, but I don't do two at a time and it's three hundred for play, four hundred for sex with a condom."

Marty clasps his hands in supplication, "don't worry Brandy, we'd like to start off by explaining why we've brought you here. There's this guy named John. He's a pizza delivery guy. We'd like you to answer the door and seduce him so he forgets about the rest of his deliveries."

She waits until her laughter subsides, "let me get this straight. You want me to pretend that I live here, and seduce your friend the pizza boy?"

I look at Marty like *I told you this wasn't a good idea*, "yeah. Forget it." I say, "It's a stupid idea."

"You got the cash?" she asks.

Marty holds out the $400 mostly in twenties and tens.

She takes the money and stuffs it in her jeans pocket with not much room to spare.

"So, you boys aren't looking for anything?"

"Well, um not really. We just want you to distract him," says Marty.

She looks nervous. Marty stammers on, "we'd like to y'know, but we gotta pay rent."

"Yeah, you *are* very beautiful," I say.

"So, when is this guy supposed to show up?"

"We haven't called yet. There are still a few details we need to go over. Here, have a seat," Marty leads her into the living room and waits for her to sit on the couch before taking a seat on the wicker deck chair opposite.

"You're an actress, right?"

She smiles, her real face becoming visibly more engaged beneath the layers of make-up, "yeah, I've been in a few plays and a commercial. I was in a magazine…"

"Great. Feel free to improvise. What I need you to do is…" Marty proceeds to tell her his entire plan, making stuff up as he goes along. He tells her to fake cry and gives her a motivation, "you're in the midst of a moral dilemma. You feel guilty for cheating on your boyfriend with the pizza boy. He's away and you're stuck at home. A lonely housewife."

The girl nods, taking his direction in earnest. Marty sits beside her on the couch, leans in for a kiss, fondles her breast, "like this," he says.

"Should I be undressed?" she asks.

"Undressed, yeah."

"Marty," I say. "Shouldn't we be getting on with it? I'mean the real deal."

"Right. I'll call him now," he says, allowing time for the swelling in his pants to go down. "Ah-ha! I've got it," ambling toward the phone, "what kind of pizza do you like Brandy?"

"Where's it from?"

"Beaufort."

A pause, "I don't really like their pizza."

"Sorry, but it has to be…"

"Mediterranean."

"You got it."

"You guys have cable here?" she asks.

"Yeah, remote's on the table," I say.

She picks up the remote and sifts through the channels while Marty dials Beaufort. "All done," he says hanging up. "He'll be here in half an hour. One Mediterranean comin' up… *and a chef special*," Marty whispers, *"that's for us."*

"Mmm hmm," she says, switching between an episode of Jerry Springer and a Swollen Members video.

"O-kay, all done here. Thanks a lot Brandy."

"Yeah, thanks a lot," I say.

"Sure guys, have yourselves a real nice evening."

Marty leaves some cash on the counter, "here's forty dollars. Given the circumstances I don't think you'll need to give him a tip."

Brandy turns and in a soothing contralto says, "It's all under control, sweetie, go on."

We leave and run to our bench on the hill furnishing a view of the living room window. The blinds are open as promised, Marty sights in the binoculars. I am just able to see her on the couch starting to get comfortable, unbuttoning her blouse. She gets up and goes to the window, probably looking for us.

"See man, John's finally gonna get what's comin' to him," says Marty, lighting up another joint. It's burned down halfway when John arrives. Marty leers through the binoculars. I can just barely make out Brandy as she strips off her shirt and bra and goes to answer the door.

"Hey, give me those," I say.

"Just a minute. Hardly anything is happening yet."

"Bullshit, you cheap son of a bitch, I paid a hundred and fifty bucks," reaching for the binoculars.

Marty leans away using his height to his advantage, "It was my idea."

John enters. Brandy pulls off her pants then her underwear and hastily discards them.

"Whoa," Marty ogles.

I jump and knock the binoculars out of his hands.

"Hey, those are expensive fucking binoculars, jerk," Marty searches for the binoculars under the flame of his lighter while I stand motionless hitting from the joint.

"Lucky they're not broken," he says, peering at the house again.

Lucky for who? I mutter to myself.

The peach schmaltz of Brandy's perfume catches in John's throat. She pulls his shirt over his head and unzips his fly. His pants fall around his knees as they shuffle towards the couch, making out to the unromantic din of Jerry's guests in the background. John succeeds in removing his pants without lifting his lips from her face and struggles to take off his underwear in similar fashion. Free of his encumbrances, he hoists her legs over his shoulders while tearing open a condom wrapper with his teeth like beat the clock. She remains impassive throughout, making only minimalist efforts to accommodate him. John's protracted breathing and jerky indecisive lovemaking leave a lot to be desired.

He sighs, his jaw drops and it's over.

The Book of John pt. 1 'The Curse of John'

With business-like composure Brandy slides off the couch and crosses the room to the window.

"Oh no! She just closed the blinds?" says Marty.

"What? Now we won't know what the hell's going on. They could be ripping me off!" I say with genuine concern.

"Nah, don't worry about it. If anything's missing, we'll call the agency."

"It'll be a little too late then, won't it?"

"We'll hide in the bushes across the street and go in as soon as John leaves. She won't have time to steal anything."

"He'd better get outta there quick. I don't trust him either."

"I've got to go to the bathroom," says Brandy.

John follows her with his eyes as she crosses the floor in front of him, "Uh, ok..." John is at even more of a loss for words than usual.

Brandy collects her clothes, accidentally sweeping John's underwear in with hers and exits down the dark, narrow hallway. The show segues into a commercial. John shifts uneasily. Pangs of alarm go off. How long has he been here? Duty calls. After a fruitless search for his underwear he puts on his shirt, pants, shoes and tracks Brandy to the end of the hall where a light shines from under a door.

"Um, Hel-lo. Sorry, but I have to be going now... Did you see my shorts, maybe you grabbed them with yours?"

The sound of weeping becomes audible.

"Are you o-kay?"

The weeping continues.

"Hel-lo?" he knocks once. "Everything okay in there?"

"Be out in a second."

The door opens, Brandy exits fully dressed. John retreats keeping a respectful distance, "did you happen to see my underwear?"

"No, were you wearing any?"

"Well, yeah."

"Did you look on the floor?" distractedly grabbing her purse and looking for things to throw in it.

"I already did."

"Sorry, hun. What do I owe you for the pizza?"

"Oh, the pizza. Oh shit. I gotta go."

"Here's twenty bucks," Brandy grabs two fives and a ten off the counter and shoves it into John's pants, feeling around inside. John clears his throat quietly, dispelling a subsequent erection.

"It was fun sweetie," Brandy opens the door.

"Can I call you?" says John.

"Just stop by. Anytime."

"What's your name?"

"Brandy."

John leans in for a kiss, her face framed in the doorway. She puckers her lips and shuts the door.

Marty and I are crouched in a ditch across the street watching John as he joggles back to the car. Changing the set of his face to one of pure business before taking off with all four cylinders screaming.

"What a bunch of bullshit," I say, storming back to the house.

Marty stops me on the stairs, "ole' Johnny must have gotten quite a shock, eh man?"

"Yeah, good for him," I say, swinging the door open.

We search every room hoping to discover her waiting in some stage of undress, but no deal. All we find is the balled up briefs on my bedroom floor.

"Shit man, I guess she went out the window," says Marty.

"Well, there you go," I say kicking the underwear at him.

"Nah, you can have 'em."

I pick them up with a fork and throw both the fork and the underwear in the garbage.

"Hey, I got a plan," he says.

"No, no no. Not interested. No more plans. Just leave. I'm pissed."

"Wait, let's phone the pizza place and complain that the pizza is cold. You can pretend you're a dissatisfied customer."

"O-kay," feeling the need to vent on someone I don't know. A man answers, I jump down his throat before he has a chance to finish his spiel. "Yeah, I finally got my fucking pizza two minutes ago and it's barely fucking edible. It's all cold and limp. I don't think it is the size I ordered either. What the fuck are you going to do about it?"

The voice tries console *me*, the irate customer, "I'm terribly sorry sir, I can send another one, what is the address?"

"2709 fucking Rock City road."

"Okay, our delivery person will be there in twenty minutes, can I have your name?"

"Gawain, Lucius Gawain."

"O-*kay*, and your phone number."

"213 4456."

"A-and what was it exactly that you ordered."

"My God man, don't you already have this down?"

"W-well our delivery person has all the bills, after the pizzas go out, we don't have any records…"

"Large anchovy, green pepper, onion and ham," slamming the phone down. "Ha-ha! Good luck, John's going to be driving around looking for a place that probably doesn't even exist."

Marty is in the living room eating pizza and watching Jerry's final thoughts, "What did you tell them?"

"To deliver it to some imaginary address on Rock City."

"Ha-ha. Good one."

I take a look at the pizza, pepperoni, mushrooms *sniff-sniff* and onions.

"Got any booze? Let's celebrate," Marty says from a reclined position on the couch.

I don't know what to do. Eat the pizza or mash it in his face.

"Hey, I just got another idea," he says.

"Of course, you do," I say, abandoning Marty to the pizza, while I go to my room and hit silently from the pipe.

Marty can be heard over sounds of smack down action, breaking glass and gunfire, "this time I'll call up and say I didn't get my pizza at all."

A few seconds later I hear him affecting a fake Hindu accent, claiming damages to his property, something about a fountain pen or an ursula gander? He orders a large Hawaiian and has it sent to another phony address.

Meanwhile Beaufort has received several calls from people saying they had not yet received their pizza.

John's boss, an otherwise mellow 20-something folk singer, lays into him the best he can as soon as he gets back from his Brandy encounter, "John, we've had quite a few complaints tonight. I'm gonna have to let you go and if you're not back here in an hour, you're not gonna get paid for tonight."

He never finds 2709 Rock City and doesn't get paid for the night.

Carla is curled up on the couch when John wanders in later than usual. He leans over to kiss her. She bends forward. A silent alarm rings somewhere far away, getting closer and closer until it fills the room. *Something's up, something's not right... and who just walked in the door?* Following her nose, she sniffs him out.

"Why do you smell like cheap fucking perfume?"

"I was delivering to this party on Rock city."

"Bullshit."

"A drunk chick."

"Bullshit."

"Rubbed up against..."

"What? She rubbed you?" Carla throws a coffee mug. It misses him by inches and slams into the wall.

"Hey, watch it," says John, making conciliatory gestures with his hands.

After an hour of clarifying his convoluted and outright lie of a story he succeeds in convincing her. The gist of it being that nobody knew where the host of the party was or whom the pizzas were for so he had to sell them individually and refuse bribes of all sorts before extricating himself.

While they are getting undressed and climbing into bed she whips a vase at the wall behind him.

"Where are your underpants John?"

"I must have forgot."

"Bullshit. Get OUT!"

John is unable to do much besides get out of the way. She chases him into the foyer, into the hall, down the stairs and into the lobby.

"Baby, don't do this." He sobs, telling her the rest of the story about getting fired, about the mix-ups and the false addresses. She gives up for the night and goes back to the apartment, vowing to break up with him and move out before the week is through.

He sneaks upstairs and to his relief finds the door open. She's in their room with the door shut. He cuts through the kitchen avoiding the hall altogether and sleeps lightly on the couch, naked, without a blanket. The next night he does the same, but has his clothes in a neat pile on the floor, a bottle of vodka and a sheet to sleep with.

The following days are spent at the music store playing expensive guitars and job-hunting, but Max won't take him back. For a while it seems that nobody wants John, but after a few reps at a new record of 300 pounds he's his old self again, determined to write the best song he's ever written, scratch that, the best song ever.

He sits out back the apartment serenading Carla until the lights go off in their room. On the morning of the fifth day Carla's mother arrives from Ontario to help her move. Mistaking it as a chance at redemption, John finds himself in a physical altercation with both of them. They beat him with kitchen utensils and call the police to take him away. He spends the night in jail and comes into the store the next morning to tell us about it. After several failed attempts at writing a new song he smashes the guitar against the stucco wall of his quondam apartment building. The only thing he can still be proud of is his make-out session with Brandy. He thinks about her until he can't think anymore. Anticipating another hot encounter, he returns to 41 Pine Street, knocks and waits patiently.

I answer.

"What are *you* doing here?"

This is one contingency I hadn't planned for. I slam the door and lock it before he has time to put the pieces together, but it wouldn't be a party without Marty so I tell him to get over here as soon as possible. I just scored an ounce and want to get him high for all the nice things he's done for me.

He says he'll be over right away.

Thanks for reading

If you enjoyed this book, please consider leaving a review wherever you saw/ read it, add it to a reading list, or go to *Goodreads* and put in a review.

You can contact me at:
books@danielthompsontheauthor.com

and/ or subscribe at:
https://www.danielthompsontheauthor.com

Read more:
https://daniel-j-thompson.medium.com

Instagram:
@thompson_dj_author

Tiktok
@daniel_j_thompson_author